PRAISE FOR
Ciao Bella

There isn't a hell of a lot I'm gonna be able to say about this book. But I'd say this is possibly my favourite Mafia book that RVD has written. To say I've loved all the Elite Eagles books and the spin-offs is an understatement, but this one is some kind of special.

—**Donna, Saucy Review On Kinky Korner**

Clear your schedule, get rid of interruptions, and hold on to your hat, because once you dive into this one, you won't be able to emerge again until the final shots are fired. With the usual mob mayhem, a river of crimson, and ridding betrayal, the twists will taunt, the turns will confound, and the secrets revealed will leave you gob smacked. If you're at all a fan of mafia romance, this exhilarating, jaw-dropping, riveting read is guaranteed to leave you breathless!

BookAddict, Goodreads Reviewer

This story has it all love, hate, laughs, family and of course mafia. All the feels with this incredible story. The ending was a masterpiece you'll definitely be asking for more.

—**Marisela M. Chavez**

I bow down to this queen… her ability to have me in a chokehold in this mafia world is unbeatable. This series owns me and I'm not mad about it… I'll happily surrender myself to this world—these characters. This is a take all my stars, must read!

—It.sgottabethebooks

Ivan and Bella's story is an emotionally riveting, epic start to the 'Rise of the De Langes' series. It's a tumultuous enemies-to-lovers, forced proximity, mafia romance teeming with suspense, clever banter, and witty threats like only the EE characters can pull off. RVD's writing, especially her mafia series, has the ability to take my breath away.

—**Melissa, Book Boyfriend and Husband Makes Three**

Rachel does it again!! Back to the mafia world and it doesn't disappoint. Ciao Bella is fantastic! There is angst, twist and turns that keep you on the edge your seat.

——**Vaneece, Goodreads Reviewer**

Ivan and Bella's hatred for each other was announced on page one, and I was instantly giddy to experience that hatred! And experience it I did! In all its beautiful glory!

—**Katy, stucknbooks**

The many twists and turns throughout this story in addition to complex characters and situations show Ms. Van Dyken's writing skills off perfectly. I love that my mind considers all the possibilities whilst reading the story. This author's narratives are always superbly written and thoroughly enjoyable.

—**Ann, Literary Lust**

GOOSEBUMPS!! I've read all the books in this mafia world, and this just somehow gave me the early days eagle elite vibes. The love hate relationship between the main characters was just felt through the pages.

—**Justmyfantasyworld**

CIAO
Bella

RACHEL VAN DYKEN

#1 *NEW YORK TIMES*
BESTSELLING AUTHOR

Ciao Bella
The Rise of the De Langes, Book 1
by Rachel Van Dyken

Copyright © 2024 RACHEL VAN DYKEN®

This is a work of fiction. Names, places, characters, and events are fictitious in every regard. Any similarities to actual events and persons, living or dead, are purely coincidental. Any trademarks, service marks, product names, or named features are assumed to be the property of their respective owners, and are used only for reference. There is no implied endorsement if any of these terms are used. Except for review purposes, the reproduction of this book in whole or part, electronically or mechanically, constitutes a copyright violation.

CIAO BELLA
Copyright © 2024 RACHEL VAN DYKEN®
ISBN: 978-1-957700-83-0

Edited by Kay Springsteen and Jill Sava
Cover & Interior Design by Jill Sava, Love Affair With Fiction

A NOTE ON
Content

Some of you like to know if there is anything in a book that may be difficult for you to read. Some real-life issues are discussed/portrayed within these pages.
If you would like to see what they are, please flip to the very last page or scan the QR Code

As always, thank you for reading!

DEDICATION

To the mighty warriors in all of us
and to knowing your worth
oh… and making them pay.

CHAPTER
One

You can't bestow wisdom on idiots. I would know. My dad told me that every day until I realized it was me. I was the idiot. God love him.
—King Campisi, Capo dei Capi

Bella

There are three things you absolutely need to know about me.

One, I have a short temper, compliments of my dad.

Two, my dad is, to put it mildly, one of the most powerful mafia bosses in Chicago.

Three, I hate ham. Can't stand it, which brings us into four.

Okay, so I meant four, whatever.

And four, I despised Ivan De Lange with every fiber of

my soul. If he was on the side of the street limping, you best believe it was because I ran him over with my car, my bike, and then a stolen tricycle for good measure.

He wasn't making matters easier by picking a fight during family dinner in front of everyone.

More yelling commenced from inside the house. I winced.

And now you're all caught up.

I'm Bella Abandonato, college sophomore at one of the most elite universities in the nation, spoiled princess, hell of a cookie lover, and this is how I destroyed my enemy: one chocolate chip at a time.

Damn, too much? And was I really trying to do my manifesto while Ivan cornered me in the yard next to the giant tree he'd pushed me out of when I was fifteen?

Yes.

Was it the same tree I shoved his head against? Also, yes.

I had no problem feeling guilty when it came to him, and he had no qualms about being guilty when it came to me.

"You're an idiot," I said with purpose and a strong sense of conviction. I wanted to carve it into his skull so that every time he saw his own face in the mirror, he'd remember like the complete dumbass that he was.

An idiot.

See? Not that hard, and sometimes for people like him, from his Family, reading may be tough, but for him it's literally something that makes a person wonder, can he even *see words?*

Ivan leaned in, too close, way too close, his green eyes penetrated mine in a way that was so severely uncomfortable that I wanted to trip him then grab the closest object and hold it high over my head. He'd of course tell my family and it would be a whole thing, the last thing we needed was more war between the Families anyway so we're taught at an early age, not to necessarily play nice, just not to get caught by any of the bosses from any of the Families.

Ivan was cruel when I first met him at fifteen, when he came into our lives and decided to start working for the Families, not that he was really given a choice as an orphan. I'd been warned to be nice because he didn't have any parents left, but he just wore his anger so much on his sleeve that the first thing he said to me when I offered him some homemade cookies was he didn't eat poison then looked me up and down and said. "You should probably cut back anyway, am I right?" He'd pinched my side and what followed was me slamming a plate against him, cookies flying everywhere and blood everywhere that, till this day, nobody's really sure where it came from.

Then again, I was in the Cosa Nostra, Italian mafia blood ran through my veins, my heart pulsed with it each beat it took and I knew that I'd either live a seminormal life or I'd be the one to wreak havoc.

I had nothing but amazing experiences around me, if you counted all of the... er, attacks. Listen, they wanted to live normal lives too, but when you're five of the most powerful and richest Families in the underground, people tend to want to take your throne or stop air from getting into your lungs.

It was a thing.

When I was little, my dad, Nixon Abandonato, a badass in his own right and boss of the Abandonato Family, would tuck me in with my blue unicorn, kiss me on each cheek and tell me how he met Mom. "You see, our Families were at war, and her parents died a bloody death, but her Grandpa never gave up and put her into hiding, and I'd loved her for forever and never forgot her, but we were from two Families who should have never connected… blood spills when there's envy."

"What's envy?"

"Means you want what someone else has and want to…" Uncle Chase walked into the room and mimed a slit across his neck.

At the time, I thought he was just being goofy, but my dad said something mean to him in Italian that I later found out meant really bad things.

That… was normal.

And while I felt bad that my Family was responsible for the killing of Ivan's, they'd been horrible humans, so did he really have to take it out on me on a daily basis?

He's been given the world despite the fact that his Family was full of complete losers. My Family gave him a literal silver spoon to redeem himself with while shoving it up their asses, no, just no.

The actual fact that I, ME, almost got kicked out of my freshman year at Eagle Elite University, ran by dearest Dad, was unthinkable! Everyone knew who I was, and he didn't give a shit, he wasn't even scared of my dad… he respected him, but he didn't pee his pants when he made eye contact.

On top of that, he was a sociopath.

I stared across the field at him. We'd been sent out back again to fight it out. The kitchen, living room, and well, even the bathrooms were off limits to us during family dinners.

And Dad said he refused to keep fixing the dents in the walls. Apparently, twice was enough.

Ugh, I hated him so much.

He grinned at me, shirtless because he knew how good he looked, tan from the summer, ready to graduate this year, muscles everywhere and his Family crest splashed in red and black across his chest with Nicolasi written beneath it.

He was a fallen De Lange and a reborn Nicolasi.

Gross.

His white shorts were hanging on for dear life, I mean, what if they just fell past that annoyingly deep V by his hips, what then?

Public indecency in my backyard?

He rolled his eyes. "Sorry, princess, the licking schedule's full for the day, so put the disgusting tongue back into your mouth before I puke into mine."

I crossed my arms. "Wow, charming. The way I'm dying to suddenly kiss you is alarming, should I just make a jump for it?"

He took a step back.

I took a step forward. "Aw, you gonna run?"

He tilted his head, crossing his bulky arms across his chest. "Not if you're chasing, might give you the wrong idea and I'm afraid if you actually get near my dick, it might fall off from all the trauma of being so close to your body. Question, did you even wash your hair today or is greasy the new thing?"

I didn't, but I'd been busy laying out in the hot sun, enjoying my last full day of summer before going back to hell to start my junior year. "I don't know charity case, at least I have hair."

My grin was pure evil while laughter sounded from the house. It was our last night together as a family, all the dads and uncles were leaving for the fall like they had been for the last three years when Ash, my cousin, took over along with my sister and her husband Junior, followed by my other cousins Valerian, Maksim and King. They were all young and married, angry, brilliant, and loved being in charge. They also somehow managed to get away with mixing more of the Family bloodlines without getting killed… so total win for them since it just made all of our Families stronger. And the old bosses?

They were there as mentors, but decided after a near bloodbath that it would be better for the second generation of leaders to prove themselves.

The Families had been at peace ever since… and apparently three years was a lot.

Ivan touched his head and glared. "That was cruel even for you, who just sneaks into a guy's dorm room and shaves down the middle of his skull! I had to shave my entire head, and you knew that my girlfriend would dump me!"

"Her accent was fake. Brits don't talk like that."

"This again…" He ran his hands through his jet-black hair. "Oh shit, King's looking outside, quick, laugh!"

"He'll be even more suspicious!" I hissed, slapping him on the arm. "Better that we just fight and get it over with. He's scary as shit these days now that he's the new Capo."

"I prefer calling him Godfather, he gets that weird twitch in his eye. Also, what was weirder he's only four years older than me and he looks like he eats squirrel raw just because they grabbed a nut from his yard, or his nuts, meh same thing, why does he hate squirrels so much again?"

I frowned. "That's what you're focusing on? Hurry, hit me!"

"I have zero death wishes, just kick me in the leg and I'll fall or something, but if you hit anywhere in between both legs, all bets are off."

I smiled. "Like you'd even feel it."

"Ha, ha. Hurry his eyes keep narrowing. I can see it from the window. Man needs a hobby other than killing and having loud enough sex that everyone can hear. I still can't stare at bread baskets without a moment of silence."

"Yeah, what's his thing with bread? It's weird."

"Or your uncle's thing with bagels?" He snorted. "Maybe they've lost their sanity, too much screaming and death, go, go, go!"

I hurried and kicked him in the shin, then did a quick takedown while he rolled me to my back. "Still there?"

Ivan exhaled, his hands gripping my shoulders. "He's still looking, head butt me, he needs to see blood."

"It's your turn this time!"

"I know, but every time I do, Junior looks like he's going to kill me even though it's normal in this world, hurry the hell up and make me bleed, bitch!"

That did it. I punched him in the mouth, hurting my knuckles in the process, while blood spurted from his lower lip. "Hurt?"

He nodded. "I can at least respect you've been hitting the gym. It didn't tickle. Congrats, you're a woman now, maybe one day you'll know what it's like to buy tampons and lose your virginity?"

I didn't give him time, I just rolled him onto his back and punched him again.

Fake fighting turned into real fighting, until we returned to family dinner, and awkwardly cleared our throats at the same time.

I had grass in my hair.

He had blood running down his chin.

The skin on my knuckles bled a bit. I smiled over at Ivan. "Dearest Ivan, can you please pass the rolls?"

"I would love nothing more, bestie."

It was business as usual.

To outsiders it may have seemed weird, but everyone just kept eating and talking, pouring wine, while I shot him glares the entire time. I chewed another bite of steak.

I kicked him under the table, causing him to choke on his bite. "Sorry, my foot was cramping."

"My. Ass." He rolled his eyes, and all was right within our world, the mafia world, the second generation of the most powerful Families in the US.

Welcome to the world of Eagle Elite.

Blood in, no out.

As burns this saint, burns my soul, I will get into this life alive, and get out dead.

Amen.

CHAPTER Two

*Family dinners are kind of like war.
Blood will always be spilled.
And the spoils will always go to the victors.
—King Campisi*

Ivan

Bella and I had just finished bleeding on the table, eating our meal, and everyone was already getting their assignments and going their separate ways so why was I the one person who was getting lectured less than twenty-four hours before I had to start senior year? I had shit to do, but if I showed my temper even more than I already had, I'd get sent downstairs.

And you did not want to meet anyone in that boxing ring, women included, hell, even the dog with the missing though it was disconcerting how many milk cow bones it looked like he was eating. I brought it up once.

And all I heard was silence and slicing through meat as knives scratched against porcelain plates.

Everything was tense until two years ago when the Five Families gave the De Lange Family—hi, that's me, orphan spawn of them—a treaty and money to rebuild what had been taken from them. Junior De Lange was the acting boss, but in one week they would vote to either stay as part of the Five Families officially, branch off, or betray everyone again. Junior had rebuilt them from the ground up and also put the fear of God in them by way of blood accidentally getting spilled, but he was good for the job—a job I would rather be buried alive than have.

So, to say things were extremely tense during family dinner when the parents and second gen bosses were present… well, to be a fly on the wall would honestly be the most interesting thing if you could avoid getting murdered by one of the many people sitting around eating and staring at their plates like the world could potentially burn down.

I cleared my throat and chose the calmest voice I could muster in response to the previous argument with Phoenix, technically my closest relative in the group and the boss of the Nicolasi Family. "For the last time, since I wasn't making myself clear, no I do not want to major in philosophy because it's too hard, I want to major in Poli Sci, come out the other end not wanting to kill myself for thinking so many thoughts and I want to follow in the Families' footsteps!" Shit, I'm yelling at Phoenix Nicolasi, I heard a guy once got his finger cut off for raising his eyebrows. Should I be petrified?

Absolutely. Shit, he's going to feed me to Serena's toddler Bam-Bam (His nickname for reasons I'm sure everyone thought but never said out loud). As if on cue, Bam-Bam half-walked half-crawled up to me and sat. Had he been wearing a kerchief, glasses, and a bow tie around his scraggly neck while holding a knife in each hand, I don't think I would have even blinked. The bosses started moving away from me. Ash, the Abandonato boss, suddenly found something interesting on the floor to stare at, Junior was staring at his dad as if to say, don't kill him. And don't even get me started on King; not a good sign when even he gulps down some wine and pours more.

Terrifying, to be correct.

I sighed. "Listen, Phoenix, I get that you feel a certain responsibility toward me because you and Chase killed my parents—" I held up my hands while Ash cursed under his breath.

"And here we go again…" Ash handed Junior a twenty. What the hell?

Serena walked into the living room and sighed, then scooted Bam-Bam's chair closer to the table and to me before putting him in his seat. Great. "Is he arguing again?"

"Yes," they all said in unison, Phoenix included.

He was only supposed to sit down with me after dinner, go over the dos and don'ts of my final year of school and then go over my training schedule while the guys made me into an assassin, see? Normal discussions with your adopted parent.

I lived with Phoenix and Bee, they took me in and protected me years ago, but that did not, however, make them my parents.

My dad was a horrible human being that deserved to be stabbed all those times in the back for what he did to my mom, to my little sister, to my dog—he even killed my pet fish, so there was no sentiment there.

But the whole concept that the same Family I swore my fealty to was actually in charge of killing half of my relatives kind of made me want to throw up—because we'd still had some good people left, and now they were cleansed, gone. I got that my relatives were part of the cursed line, as Ash so eloquently put it, but things were different now.

Things were calm.

We had a new Capo.

I had friends.

Serena even bought me a fish and named it blue. I was one of the youngest De Lange's still left, but I'd done a damn good job fighting for the Five Families, so why couldn't I at least choose what I majored in?

I even stopped hiding under the kitchen table when I heard loud noises—bad habit from when my mom and dad would fight—they liked to throw things—the point was—I could handle it now. I was twenty-one and after taking a gap year and going to Italy to attempt to find myself and also learn how to… possibly, become an assassin like the other guys, I did find myself.

It was called staring at your reflection via your shiny dagger, and it was perfection. I also found several girls who agreed with that sentiment, over and over and over—you get the picture.

Phoenix sighed and hung his head. He looked like he was just cast on the show Vikings with his shaved sides and long brown hair braided back. It took one minute for his wife Bee to see him in a Halloween costume as a Viking and it was all over, he'll never do his hair different again; I heard blood was shed, but that's not just typical for Viking mentality but for the Family.

"Why?" Phoenix rubbed down his face with both hands and pulled the tie from his neck and opened up his black button-down shirt. "Why do kids never listen?"

"He's not a kid," Junior piped up. "You're just losing your edge and getting protective."

Phoenix's head snapped toward his son. "Care to repeat that?"

"Nope." Junior took a step back. "All I'm saying is, the only reason you want him to major in Philosophy is because in your head it's safe, but guess what? Nobody is safe, we're never safe, I mean dipshit over there"—he pointed at Ash—"ran into a wall because he was watching a TikTok!"

"You promised!" Ash yelled.

Junior snorted. "Oh please, you were watching the Barbie dance again and wondering how Ken got so tan when he's not even Italian."

"Is there any other option anymore other than getting sent under the bus by a cousin, peer, parent?" Serena sighed.

"To the mattresses," Ash added.

"My. God." Phoenix kicked the couch, then adjusted it since he knew his wife would most likely notice and ask why he was using his anger, not his words. They were a riot. "Is it so bad that I want to keep you safe, Ivan?"

I winced. "I'm safe, consider me completely safe, I mean, have you looked around you?" I pointed to the living room full of bosses and assassins. "Between the OG mafia bosses—" I grimaced when Chase walked in and narrowed his eyes at me. "No offense."

"All of it is taken, but continue," Phoenix said.

I smiled. "And the new bosses, all your sons, might I add—Junior put your hand down we know he's your dad."

Junior winked at me. "Just trying to make it more awkward."

"Literally all he does," Ash said under his breath, earning a swift kick in the ass from Junior's boot and a take down from behind compliments of Serena.

Chase shook his head and walked right back out of the living room. "Children."

"All I'm saying..." I ignored the brawl taking place next to me and saved the crystal vase, lifting it into the air before the table went flying. "...is that, you've trained me well, and I have several friends plus at least three of our guys actually work at Eagle Elite, so no, I don't need to take philosophy so that I'm in the safe non-business classes and no it's not going to convince me to take my own path. I'm in it, blood in no out, you could send me to knitting—"

"—Don't hate on knitting," King said under his breath. "It's a very soothing process."

"Anyway..." I ignored him. "Even if I took the wonderfully soothing process of a knitting class."

King gave me what felt like a very sarcastic thumbs up that also somehow managed to communicate that I was seconds away from getting punched.

"I would still be part of this Family and part of this world, so could you just give me a break, let me enroll in my own classes, run my own life and stop shoving your business up my ass?"

"Oh shit," Junior said before pulling away from Ash.

"I'm just going to be outside… the house, touching grass."

"I need grass," Ash added.

"Not that kind of grass, dumbass." Junior grunted.

Serena was the last to leave, taking Bam-Bam with her.

I thought my argument would maybe be over.

I thought everything would be fine.

And then footsteps sounded. Bella had cleaned up the blood and put on a pair of low-slung black sweats and a matching tight black tank top. Was she even wearing a bra? Did she want to die so young? Good, my nemesis was going to get a free show.

She jerked her head toward the kitchen as if to remind me of the Ivan-Bella Rules taped to the fridge and gave me a pointed look.

As a joke, not funny by the way, Chase made them into metal signs for everyone so they could keep them in their houses as a reminder that misbehaving earns punishment.

The first one rule was established after the Kitchen incident—lots of ice cream, a tragically broken freezer and a knife: Always stay three feet apart.

Do not bring weapons to family dinner or picnics.

Never play Hungry Hippo. You would think that one would be self-explanatory, but people always asked why.

Use only kind words, no expletives when addressing one another—this was a really hard one for both of us, so we ended up developing our own language after watching Friends in an attempt to see what the fuss was all about. I sided with Joey, I really did. Anyway, if I gave her a thumbs up it meant F you, if I gave her a thumbs down, it meant, eat shit and die, and any time either of us gave the double thumb up or down it basically meant, we were probably both packing and in genuine need to brawl. Thumbs up was let's go fight, thumbs down was if you approach me I'll end you.

I didn't mind the double thumbs up because it meant I faced her in the ring and I really didn't mind the double thumbs down because it meant we were going to compete at something to get all the anger out, victor took all. Between archery, axe throwing, swimming, and her genius idea of a barre workout, we were able to at least get some of the aggression out of our systems in a semi-healthy way, while still insulting and competing against each other.

Over the years, they've made new signs, added in more and more rules. Not excluding us, just literally avoiding eye contact.

We provoked each other in the worst way; she grew up a mafia princess with a spoiled little attitude and still thinks she's a badass because her dad trained her and I grew up the pauper nobody that had to be taken in because her dad was the great Nixon Abandonato, her uncle was Senator Chase Abandonato—she was untouchable, and she was the reason for the pain I lived in.

Her.

She also would randomly wear polka dots, then walk by me and ask if I was dizzy—so she purposefully dressed to piss me off. No girl that hot should be that cruel. And the worst part? She was the youngest, so she constantly got away with it.

She could sneeze out a fart then commit murder, say sorry and people would say, "Aw, baby girl, did you have a hard day? Should I wipe your ass for you?"

I gritted my teeth and looked away.

"You guys already drew blood today. Remember the

rules." Phoenix stated in that bored tone that meant I wasn't allowed to argue, let alone fail at anything in life. He stared down at his folded hands and wrung them together, it wasn't something I could say I noticed a lot, but when he was really stressed and trying to keep it in or keep the violence in, he did that.

I would never admit it out loud, but I hated knowing it was my fault and in moments like that, I really did want to reach out and say sorry, but all that ended up coming out was sarcasm.

A few seconds beat by. "They're tattooed on my soul." I grunted out. "The rules, that is."

In typical Bella fashion, she honest to God twirled into the room like the picture of innocence, her long dark hair fell near to her waist like she was channeling Rapunzel and her bright green eyes roamed across every piece of furniture only to glaze past me and land on Phoenix. "Shocked, he still has one, am I right?"

"Bella." His tone got even lower; I didn't think it was actually possible.

She marched right up to him and reached out. Her touch was gentle, her fingers grasped his arm, then his hand. You've got to be shitting me. "Did you need me for something?"

Could she suck up any more? What the ever-loving FBI or CIA secret shit was she on?

Phoenix melted on the spot, his eyes softened, even his body seemed to relax, as his jaw unclenched. He honestly didn't look happy about her little trick but still managed to pull her in for a hug, his lips brushed the top of her head in a swift kiss. I rolled my eyes. "Disgusting."

Bella turned and looked over her shoulder, flipping her

hair dangerously close to my person. "It's called affection, but you wouldn't know that if I spelled it out for you and tattooed it on that missing soul of yours a million times, do you even know how to hold someone's hand? It's like you're allergic to touch, and feelings, and anything remotely fun! It wouldn't kill you to smile without murder on your mind."

"I'm fun!" I argued.

"Rule number seven," Phoenix barked.

"Fine," we said in unison.

I crossed my arms, probably more aggressive than needed.

She crossed hers, mimicking me to perfection as she always did.

And Phoenix just stared between the two of us. "You'll both be attending school starting tomorrow. Look out for one another... I'm adding a new rule to the millions of rules you have between each other. Family sticks together. If someone as much as blinks at Bella, you warn them away, if she gets attacked you kill them no questions asked and Bella if anyone bullies him or says anything about his family line, you kick them in the balls, you both have your strengths in combat and in what I can only say is manipulation to the extreme. Family is blood, now give me your hands and give me your vows."

"Does that mean I can major in—" I stopped talking. Phoenix wasn't playing any games. Instead, I walked over and gave him my hand.

Bella gave him hers.

Phoenix grabbed the dagger from his back pocket and, without any warning, slid it across Bella's palm.

She didn't even flinch.

Two could play that game.

I swear my cut was deeper. As intense burning pain made itself known and blood started running down my wrist. I watched as it slid down my forearm. Phoenix grabbed both of our hands and pressed our palms together, aggressive even for him. "Be nice. Get along. Don't kill each other. You aren't the enemies; the people out there are."

It was abrupt, the drop of our hands like he was washing his own clean. He walked between us, stepping in droplets of blood, and muttered over his shoulder. "Clean up your mess."

It was a double meaning; we both knew that.

Clean up the blood.

And clean up the brokenness and hatred between us, but some things were easier said than done, some scars you purposefully keep fresh because what the hell would happen if they healed?

"Yeah, Ivan, clean up the mess," Bella said, mentally slapping me out of my own morose thoughts and insecurities, it was her gift, and it made the anger even stronger, the hatred that I could never fully grasp. I knew I felt it, and I directed it at her, but I never truly knew why it bothered me so much which bothered me more, because then I wondered if there was something innately wrong with me, my bloodline, my personality, and then the thoughts went to...

You're. Just. Like. Them. The De Langes, and one day, you'll prove it right and the castle will crumble beneath your feet, leaving nothing but dust.

Phoenix stopped at the door. "Bella, rule number fourteen."

"No provoking Ivan," she said under her breath.

Looking over his shoulder, Phoenix said, "Get along or

I'll have both your heads, and Bella, I don't care that Nixon's my best friend, he'd encourage it, you've been spoiled way too long. It's time to grow the hell up."

With that, he left the living room. The silence was deafening. We'd pushed him too far—we'd pushed all of them too far, and for what? Rage built up in my soul when I stared down at the drops of blood on the carpet, I had only one choice in order to tamper it down, the abandonment and the very real feel of blood being on my own hands and never being enough no matter what I did, not having a life despite lives being taken from me, no identity outside of what I was born into. I blamed her. I looked at her and thought to myself that somehow it was her fault, her Family's fault, and I clung to it, because looking inside was too hard. I flashed her a smirk. "Think OxiClean will do it or not?" I stepped on it and smushed it into the carpet. "Maybe you should hurry up and get on your hands and knees? Should be pretty natural for you, though I am curious… do you close your eyes or keep them open?"

"I loathe you." She grabbed the rag and rubbed it further into the carpet with her tall black boot, refusing to get on her knees like I knew she would.

I instantly snapped and grabbed her by the thigh, digging my fingers into her leg and flipped her onto her back, pinning her to the carpet and against the blood, good, let it mix with her perfection. "I think you have a new stain on your shirt now, little girl."

She tried kneeing me in the balls and flipping me over.

Footsteps sounded. "Son of a bitch, rule sixteen!" Nixon yelled.

"Sorry Daddy." She tried to roll out from underneath me.

"I'll be your daddy." I leaned down and whispered in her ear, just to piss her off.

It wasn't long, maybe five seconds, before cold water was dumped on both of us.

Shit!

Bella's scream was almost worth it.

I scrambled back, Nixon tossed the bucket on the ground. "Play nice."

And then he was gone.

CHAPTER Three

The calm before the storm is more terrifying than the storm itself.
—King Campisi

King

"They're getting bolder, that's for sure," Junior muttered as he tossed a blood-soaked shirt onto the table.

I tilted my head and examined it. His dark hair was longer now, messy, also covered in blood, I wasn't sure if it was his or someone else's, as the Capo, the new leader of the Five Families I was almost afraid to ask.

Maksim was dealing with the Sinacore side of things, which left me here with the remaining few.

Santino helped out with the Petrov Family under Valerian, while Junior kept the shit that was the De Lange

Family and all of their missing pieces together.

The Alfero's were the easiest since Dante had them pretty much sedated with so much money coming in that it was borderline embarrassing… as long as people got paid, they forgot past grievances, wonders never ceased. Dom basically floated around but mainly stayed on to help Junior with the chaos that was the De Langes.

I was probably missing a dozen people at this point… it didn't matter too much since everyone worked so cohesively, including my Family. And mine? The Campisi throne was running like a fine-tuned machine.

Often it felt like we were too young to lead, but we proved to our parents we were ready, just like they had proved (in bloodshed) to their own that they were ready. Ours was more of a *it's our turn, back off* mentality.

And they let us, slipping into cheerful retirement yet still looking like they were in their thirties ready to pop out more kids.

I shuddered. "What's with the blood?" I finally asked Junior.

He shrugged. "Men keep killing each other, so I keep killing them to keep them from killing each other. It's math."

Ash burst out laughing. "Math was literally your worst subject."

"Eat shit." Junior groaned into his hands. "Ninety percent of the De Langes are loyal, they want to re-establish more than their own name, we've built up the ranks to what they were before, but something seems off, some of the men seem… too arrogant, too unafraid of me, and I've given them plenty of reasons to be petrified."

"Please list them and in graphic detail," Maksim said in a

bored tone. Ah, good, he was back into his other personality, where he wanted to hear all about the darkness so he could feed his soul.

It was still weird to me at times that he had two personalities, also known as dissociative identity disorder, then again, at times I think it helped him compartmentalize all of his past memories along with things he'd had to do in order to survive.

Valerian ran his hands through his light brown hair, a new black tattoo was etched near his thumb, the guy only got ink if something bad or good went down, I made a mental note to ask later. "Listen, I need to get home, if there are no more updates…" He started to stand.

"We're at peace."

Santino, Maksim, Ash, Junior, and Valerian all glanced in my direction. My voice wasn't confident like it normally was.

Santino groaned into his hands. "You Americans and your fears. We're at peace, you should drink wine and be happy."

"Says the assassin that had to flee his own Family," Maksim muttered under his breath.

"For good reason." Santino pointed out. "Plus, someone had to save your sorry asses."

"Boo." Junior gave us a giant thumbs down. "Don't act so pretentious, little Italy, it makes us think you're working with a small dick."

"How old are you again?" Santino asked.

Junior grinned. "Old enough to kick your ass, young enough to survive if you try to kick mine."

Ash nodded. "Yeah, that's fair. See, he can math!"

"God." Maksim hung his head in his hands. "Can't we just go home? We don't have any more threats, things have gone silent, most of us have very attractive women to go home to, some even have tiny little villains they claim as their children."

All of us turned to Junior.

He flipped us off. "Bam-Bam just has strong feelings!"

"I still think he's going to try to murder you in your sleep, but whatever," Ash said cheerfully.

"Okay, person who named their son Walt," Junior said under his breath.

"Take it back!" Ash jolted to his feet. "It's a family name!"

"From the fifties?" I asked. "Sorry, it's a great strong name. One of killers and thieves."

"Thank you." Ash sat back down.

I turned to Junior again. "What's your feeling on your men, on your stability?"

Junior swallowed. "My head tells me I'm being paranoid, but something isn't sitting right with the Family, it's like fear isn't present anymore despite this shit," He shoved the bloody shirt off the table. "It's like they think someone's going to protect them and that someone isn't me, they know I'd take them out before they could take themselves or any of the other Families out."

I tapped my fingers against the table in thought. "When does the treaty for welcoming them back into the Family end?"

"A week." Junior sighed. "Basically, if I was a narcissistic, power-hungry idiot, in a week I could be like thanks for the money and support but no thanks, I think I'm going to war against the rest of the Cosa Nostra and see how that checks out. Seriously though, most of them are young and stupid, none of them have the balls to do it."

We fell quiet until Junior whispered again, "I mean, unless… Ivan, but he doesn't even want to be a part of this life. He has more money than he needs, so what would be the purpose?"

Ash exhaled. "Revenge? Or maybe just to piss us off."

"No." I disagreed. "He's not that stupid, I mean, stupidity does run thick in all our blood, but I highly doubt he'd go that far, plus it would be a complete death sentence."

Maksim was quiet before he tapped his fingertips slowly against his thigh and reached for his glass of whiskey, taking loud but small sips before saying, "Maybe death is what he seeks."

CHAPTER
Four

Day one Sophomore and Senior year at HELL also known as Eagle Elite University. Good luck suckers.
—King Campisi

Bella

"Why?" I glared at Ivan and really made a point to make the glare look terrifying despite the fact that he'd always won on the scary side of things. Maybe it was the fact that he had these perfectly sculpted, albeit heavyish, eyebrows that framed those green eyes, it didn't help that his lashes were dark and long making every stare seem intense, at one point I just gave up and assumed his sad and happy face were the same as his angry one because of those stupid eyes.

He stared back, his expression completely unreadable, he

"This." I pointed at his motorcycle, it was a Ducati, had red and white stripes and I often wondered how pissed he'd be if I just set it on fire, it was loud, I hated loud noises that made no sense and honestly, I hated him so that actually did make sense. "Why do I have to get on this to go to college with you when I know full on you would probably crash on purpose just to injure me? This isn't safe."

Most motorcycles were safe when sane people drove them, clearly Ivan did not fall into that category. Ever. He was reckless in a way that didn't protect people, he literally didn't give a shit if dead bodies were littering the street. Some people just had no souls. Besides, everyone left early that morning, so I had nobody to complain to except for the younger cousins since the older cousins and my sister were all getting ready to do their jobs, you know, save the world from crime—haha, funny joke and nobody was in my head or the garage to hear it. Damn.

"Ah safe." He smirked, the dimple on the side of his right cheek deepened like it knew I would stare for at least a second, making it impossible to look away. "Yes, because that's what the mafia is, safe…" He tossed me the black helmet. I caught it with one hand and pulled it close to my chest. "Put it on, grab your backpack, strap on your heels and stop complaining. I actually want to participate in school and in the Family business, you can go to Hell for all I care."

I hated it when he talked down to me like I was the trophy wife of the mafia, when my only goal one day was to be called boss and crush my enemies with the latest designer heel.

"You can suck shit!" I yelled, ready to throw the helmet

at his face and see how much blood I could gain from that one small action. He had to know how much he set me off in every single human way.

Ash came out of the house and shoved his hands into the pockets of his black trousers, his matching jacket and shirt just made him look even more like the devil. His lip piercing and tattoos on his neck made a person wonder if he actually sold his soul to the devil to look like a tatted-up vampire, sometimes he looked more like Nixon's son than Chase's then other times when he dressed up he looked like a dirty politician with way too much money and time on his hands, well that and blood, always blood. "Do I need to find the bucket your dad used on you? Because it looked fun, and I woke up a bit… bored."

"Yes!" we screamed in unison. Ivan narrowed his eyes at me, and I flipped him off down by my hips so my cousin couldn't see.

Ash took a deep breath, like he suddenly needed the patience of every saint in the world. "You need to behave, remember the rules, don't make me come over and put the fear of God into that school—again. No fighting on the lawn—Serena and Junior already took care of that a few years back—be nice, pave the way for your other cousins and stop being such spoiled little shits."

He yelled the last part.

I winced.

Ivan looked away; it was the first time in months I'd seen a flicker of shame in his body language.

Ash turned around and slammed his hand on the side of the wall. "Seriously. So ungrateful." He lowered his head like he'd failed us somehow and started walking off, only to turn back around and jab a finger in our direction. "Do you realize the empire we've built for you? The safety the last few years have created? And you're arguing over helmets and motorcycles. Grow up and grow a pair." He said that last part with fervor toward Ivan. "I'm serious, otherwise neither of you are going to inherit anything. We talked about it last night at our weekly meeting. You both get nothing if you can't figure out at least a mild friendship. I'm not asking you to cure cancer, I'm asking you to be actual humans, which should be easy, but apparently after the last few days, you'd think I was praying for a miracle."

Ivan started shifting on his feet. "Ash, I just want—"

"I literally give zero shits what you want, Ivan. I know you can do better, and I know Bella makes you want to jump off a cliff, same as I know Bella wants to provoke you to the point of driving you insane, but this business doesn't call for your stupid games. It calls for seriousness and dedication, loyalty—"

He stopped and looked down. "—Maybe this is my failure as a boss."

Ivan stepped forward. "Ash, no, it's not you, it's us, it's me, I'll take full responsibility."

I rolled my eyes even though guilt crept in, Ash was only five years older than him, and he respected him a lot. "Yes agreed, we both take responsibility, and we'll try harder."

Ash looked between the two of us intensely for at least a minute before nodding his head. "You know what? New plan."

Oh Hell. Ash always had the worst plans. When his wife gave birth to their first kid, his "plan" was to ask Chase to call in a favor and make sure the secret service would be at the hospital, just in case. Chase laughed at his son. Ash repeated the request, weirdly enough on top of at least fifty of the Abandonato men being stationed there, two Secret Service made their way to the front proving yet again the power our Family had even over the government. The President sent flowers. Weirdest thing I'd ever witnessed.

"You're moving into the dorms." He nodded, more to himself than us, like he'd already decided. "And you're going to stay together, in the same room, fighting it out until you can finally learn to get along, no escape routes, no separate houses."

Had pigs literally flown in front of my face, I would have been less shocked. "I'm sorry, what? You want us to cohabitate? In actual peace?"

We struggled with family dinner, and we were placed on opposite ends of the table for a very, very legitimate reason.

Knives.

Ivan held up his hands in surrender. "I would rather stab myself in both eyes, get a root canal without shots, and crawl into my own grave that I dug myself and eat the blood-soaked dirt, so thanks but no thanks."

"Oh good," Ash said, "Be right back, I think I have some extra spots where you can start your own burial, might even have a shiny shovel and why go to the dentist when I can pull your teeth directly from your mouth, more blood that way, and I hear it mixes well with dirt, as for your eyes, well, have at it, let me know when you're ready." He stomped past us through the open garage, we both followed while he dug his hands into soft scary looking brown dirt, grabbed it and threw it in Ivan's face and grabbed a knife from the inside of his jacket, it was more machete than knife honestly.

"Eat it, but no matter how many times you do, you're still doing this, I'm sick and tired of both of you being such an issue, like I said, grow the hell up, be the solution, not the problem, you want to be made? The only way you"—he jabbed his finger at Ivan—"will ever be made in this Family, is if you get along with her and you…" I jolted at the way he thrust his finger in my face. "…need to learn humility in a huge way. I know Nixon raised you better than this, but you've been privileged and spoiled, it stops now. Pack your shit tonight and enjoy your first day at Eagle Elite. Don't kill each other." He walked off, while Ivan dusted the dirt from his face. "I almost thought he was going to break down and start quoting pop culture, then ask where he went wrong," Ivan said in a horrified voice.

I snorted out, "Yup, and it doesn't even seem weird because we're about to go to war for an entire year, we've clearly pushed him beyond his emotional and physical abilities, which says we're the worst."

"I snore." Ivan threw out. "I also sleep naked."

"I also sleep naked and snore."

"Why does this feel like war?" He turned to me, his sneer evident all over his stupid, beautiful face.

I didn't even glance back as I put on the helmet and whispered, "Because it is." I gave him a shove. "Now wash the dirt off your face, we'll come back later and pack. I don't want to be late for class and knowing Ash, he's already calling the University to make arrangements for our dorm."

Ivan paled. "Shit, we do not want to end up on the north side of campus, they only have six showers on the second floor."

My eyes widened. "I try to block out the memory of when the freshman set rats loose."

I ran back to get my helmet.

"The crickets."

I made a face. "I honestly thought the turkey run was a good idea, but they always put the loud ones in there and I need my—"

"Beauty rest?" he offered.

"Obviously not." I snorted.

"You do own a mirror, right?"

"You do own a dick, right?" I got on the bike behind him and slid my hand down his thigh. "Nah, probably not… otherwise, you'd have more balls."

"Hold tight." He ignored me. "I'm riding this as hard as someone would ride you if you were marginally attractive."

"Bite me."

"I like my mouth clean, thank you."

Ah, the joy of the first day.

We'd be lucky to be alive in the next thirty.

CHAPTER
Five

NEVER SAY NEVER. AND NEVER DOUBT SOMEONE BORN OUT OF BLOOD. THEY MAY ACTUALLY THRIVE FROM IT.
—KING CAMPISI

Ivan

Staring up at the giant brick building of torture did not give a person warm fuzzies, if anything, I was wondering how long it would take before Bella quite literally tried to come up with a solid plan to shove me off the roof.

She'd say she slipped.

I'd be a splat on the concrete.

What did I ever do to her that she hates me so much? I mean, I had a slight clue… Furthermore, why did she annoy me so much other than how spoiled she was and the embarrassment that I had always been secretly jealous of her?

I had to play nice, but the Abandonato Family was single-handedly the reason most of my Family died. I knew they deserved it, but blood was blood, it was engrained in me to be loyal to your blood, no matter how crazy it sounded, just another reason they made us swear fealty with blood—it made us one.

Gross.

"Huh." Bella pointed up at the same building. "Wonder if they keep the rooftop locked, might be a place to go and think."

"About death, yes, all ten seconds before it came for you."

"Dramatic much? Falls are messy, not enough torture, you know? I'm more of a slow poison or locking you on the roof and starving you to death sort of person."

Do I invest in safety equipment and extra food, shit she had a tendency to get dark. Pretty sure her dad had a harness somewhere and I know for a fact Phoenix had a shit ton of rope I could steal, it's stored in what I'd like to call, the dungeon right next to some shady looking machetes, several knives, and a noose that he often uses so blood isn't technically on his hands.

And that's just storage dungeon number one, his entire basement was a compound of torturous delights, though there was one room reserved for him and Bee.

I'd never asked, nor did I even want to know.

Ah, already planning on warfare on my first day back. Should that ever be a question you ask yourself in college? Yes? No? Maybe?

I needed coffee.

I checked my phone as we started walking in to the dorm, people gave us a wide birth. I almost rolled my eyes, they were so impressed with our money, good looks, ability to make people shit their pants, it's like we weren't even human anymore.

A few of the other De Lange cousins who I rarely talked to were in the same dorm, they were in training though, none of them were made—they hadn't had their first few kills, they hadn't earned it.

And they sure as hell hadn't earned it the same way I had, but that was a secret, one only Junior knew about, one he said to keep until the right time. I never questioned his motives after that moment, the rest of the Families thought I'd never spilled blood.

Another reason Phoenix was so hellbent on saving me via philosophy, he had no clue I'd been doing shit for his own son for years-and had blood-stained nightmares because of it.

"Do it." Junior handed me the knife. "He betrayed you, he betrayed us, the Family, and betrayal is betrayal."

I didn't remind him I was only eighteen, or that I was born out of blood and terrified of what would happen to me if I set the rage free. I was a De Lange after all, I'd heard rumors that the De Langes became addicted to blood, addicted to the adrenaline that followed after taking a life and obsessed with more.

Phoenix, his father, watched from the corner of the room, he was staring hard at a black folder and then back at his phone. Were his hands shaking? It was supposed to be a training exercise after all, what do you do in this sort of situation?

I'd never seen him looked stressed or confused; he was both. I kept staring, yes, he was clearly both in a way that sent chills down my spine.

Junior suddenly smacked me in the back of the head with the hilt of the knife. "Look at me, not him. Do your job prove your worth to a dying Family who might one day need you to take the reins."

My head jerked up. It was the first time he'd said something like that to me before. He was fearless, and he was the interim boss, why would he even say that out loud?

Something in his eyes flashed. A warning? A premonition?

I glanced over at the De Lange men not so casually watching.

Phoenix excused himself from the room. "We can end here, Junior, you know what to do."

I was ready to hand the knife back, but when the metal soundproof door clicked shut with such damning finality, it was hard to breathe. Junior's head tilted to the side, sizing me up, eyes narrowing, a cruel smile spread across his face. "If you want to prove you're De Lange, you have your chance, you either rise or you fall, what are you going to choose, because everyone in this Family must make a choice, rise out of the fire or be the fucking one who caused it."

"You don't need to rise if you're already there, I'd rather start the fire and watch the world burn." I knew what I had to do.

Because Junior simply smiled and stepped back as if to say, do the honors, I beg of you.

I refused any more hesitation and took the knife from him and walked behind the guy on his knees. His gag was shoved so deep into his mouth he had spit soaking it, tears ran down his face, it was hardly recognizable. He wasn't just stealing money; he was selling drugs laced with Fentanyl, something our Family never dealt with—at least not anymore.

The De Langes, for the most part, ran clean businesses now. But there was always one outlier. In every walk of life, you would always, no matter what, find the one person who thought they were the exception, not the rule.

Note, Exhibit A.

He stared up at me, his dark eyes were lost, and when he looked around the room for support that I didn't see and felt every single man look away.

I'm sure he had accomplices, people who earned money from him, but he was the fall guy.

I leaned down and whispered in his ear, "The only way out is death—say hi to my father." I slit his throat as fast as I could, warm blood spilled over my knuckles as he toppled forward, staining my white converse and blue jeans.

"Clean up." Junior tossed me a towel. "Marco, you take care of the rest with Tank."

I walked past him, then Phoenix, who gave me a blank stare before taking the cement stairs one by one up to the top, where all the happy existed.

Family. Food. Love.

The basement was for punishment.

But the kitchen? That was all reward. It was warm there. Alive.

It reminded me of my mom, most of the memories were tarnished with blood and killing, and with that, darkness, but I still remember the smell of fresh bread.

My greedy inhale was almost too loud to my own ears.

No bread, but they were cooking something with a lot of garlic.

"Hey." Serena, Junior's wife, looked over her shoulder. "What are you doing?"

I stared down at my blood-soaked shoes, still seeing the guy's lifeless body and the knife in my hand, the one that took the life.

"Training." Surviving. Staying alive. Part of me wondered, was it him or me? I would always choose me.

Junior came up next to me once she turned around and drove a knife directly into my side, maybe two inches in. Warm blood drizzled down my skin while a burning pain hit so hard I almost lost composure. "Welcome to the Family, blood in…" He jerked the bloody knife away from my skin. "…no out. You've just been made."

He walked over to his wife like the world was normal, while mine had just gone dark. My vision blurred. I was stained. I'd taken from this world.

Me or them.

I'd told them I wanted to be a part of them.

I didn't understand how heavy a wish it was.

Or how dead I would already feel.

Be careful what you wish for.

Real. So real.

"Gonna go change." I muttered and walked around the corner, where Bella nearly rammed into me. She righted herself, using my shoulders, then looked down.

We were quiet.

We were probably going to fight like we always did.

Instead, she grabbed my hand and said, "Come on."

She pulled me into her room and sat me gently on the bed, then slowly took off my shoes and put them in the trash while I held my side, it throbbed in pain; it was purposeful, that scar. I wasn't stupid. It was close enough to my back to remind me of people coming after me, and close enough to my stomach to remind me that some people stab you right in front of your face. It was the new way of becoming a made man, a constant reminder.

I was numb at that point.

Her eyes scanned over my jeans before she sighed and went into her attached bathroom and turned on the bath. The water could have been cold, hot, the bath could have been broken, I didn't even care. I just existed in that moment with blood streaming, with my nerves on end, knowing it was probably the end of something and the beginning of something even more terrifying, but I couldn't move.

Still numb, I stayed there, hands shaking.

Minutes, maybe even years later, she was pulling me to my feet and stripping me down. I still only remembered going into that bathtub and sitting. At one point, I think she tried helping wash me.

And then I remembered grabbing her, yelling at her, feeling ashamed she was seeing me that way and asking her to leave, or demanding it. In my dreams I felt her mouth on mine, my hands on her body, but I told myself it was my imagination, I told myself I would never, and yet at times the shameful part of me wondered if I did. Did I steal more than one life that night? Did I take a kiss? Did I steal her mouth again and again in order to suck some life from her that I desperately needed and did the last shred of goodness I had just disintegrate between our tongues?

Our relationship, or what was a small shroud of friendship, disappeared after that night and I still had no clue what I'd done so horribly other than being traumatized that I'd killed.

We were true enemies after that.

And now we were going to be in the same dorm room. Great. She was probably going to get back at me for it, at some point, it would only make sense.

She'd been tainted by me.

She'd tried to help.

But the only thing I'd been able to do with my voice was yell at her, but I'd needed someone to blame.

And it's always easier to blame those you secretly respect than yourself.

CHAPTER
Six

Don't ever try to fight a losing battle. No matter how many times you convince yourself it's going to work, it won't. And in the end if love is involved, good luck.
—King Campisi

Bella

It was all meaningless.

I hated that I woke up thinking that thought… it's all meaningless, like why do I even try with this guy? Every word I said was offensive to him, and every response he gave to me was so bitter that I was instantly triggered to the point of lunging at him.

My brain went back to the night things shifted—the night they changed between us, the night he still never admitted to happening, which just pissed me off even more because it made him a dirty liar.

"Can't," Ivan whispered. *"Leave. I can't."*
"I can." I fought him, and then I jumped into the bath with him. He wrapped me in his arms and cried, and then he kissed me.
It was my first kiss.
It was full of anger and pain.
And all I could do was accept it, drink it and swallow it away into the darkness where it belonged.
He was hurting and if by giving him my mouth, I could make him feel slightly better, I would.
And I did.
He pulled my shirt over my head.
He was already naked, his eyes crazed, wild, when he bit down on my shoulder and gripped my arms.
I screamed out in pain.
He shoved me away. "Go, just go!"
"Ivan—"
"—go!"

I flipped onto my back, every sound he made, every sigh, every movement in his bed made me want to murder him, it was like he was doing it accidentally on purpose—annoying me, making me question everything, doubt, and then rage.

Maybe that was the issue I truly had at the end of the day, the rage. We'd been in the dorm—the south dorms, thank God—for less than twenty-four hours and I was already glaring at him and hoping he'd actually feel said glare in his sleep.

He lied about the snoring.

He looked like a sleeping god, which quite honestly made it so much worse than him being loud. I never actually asked the universe this, but why were the pretty ones such assholes? Were his good looks to make up for his lack of personality? Was he cursed? Was I cursed for having to both stare at him and put up with him?

Ivan tossed on his left side and ran his hand through his hair. I quickly looked away like I was doing something wrong, only to look back over my shoulder in an attempt to convince myself why he was the absolute worst.

His eyebrows were clearly too sharp just like his jawline, who actually liked someone that perfect?

His chin was obviously too—obvious just poking out there like he was Gaston from Beauty and the Beast, but a way better looking version, and his fingertips were full like his stupid eyebrows and lips.

His knuckles were scarred from beating the shit out of everyone and everything, see? Welcome rage once more. His full lips pressed together in a dreamlike smirk, and I was once again angry that he existed—not only to torment me, but to make me feel inferior.

Ivan sighed again and turned toward me. The universe decided it would be an obviously good time for the sheet to fall down to his hips. Nope. I jerked away and glared at the opposing wall.

He had nothing.

I had everything.

Maybe I'd been too spoiled, too spoon-fed, too young? Who knew, but at the end of the day, he wouldn't matter to me, he was a means to an end, not even a friend.

And he'd never know the real reason why I hated him so much, just like I'd probably never know why he provoked me in the same way. We were on opposing teams in my book.

So, at the end of the day, when you took everything individually into mind, that just meant annoying and not beautiful as far as his features, which was perfectly fine by me because he already lost when it came to personality.

Then again, I tilted my head, if you took it all into one huge screen of focus like if you expanded the picture on an iPhone…

He was a god that had been placed in the wrong family line, so whatever you thought you understood—you would never trust.

De Langes, after all the stories I'd heard from my Family, were always a risk, and my only goal being the youngest daughter of the Abandonato Family was to be both ruthless…

And safe, unlike my sister and brother-in-law.

Safe also included protecting my heart at all costs.

A nice communications major I could deal with.

An accountant.

A lawyer.

Hell, even a police officer.

Maybe I was broken because the last thing I wanted was the bad boy, the forgotten, the forbidden.

"Stop." Ivan's raspy groan made me still in my bed. "You keep looking at me and then not looking at me, sighing, then looking at me again. I know I'm attractive, but God, you move so heavily in your sleep, just like the way you walk."

I jolted up and glared at him. "I'm sorry, what's wrong with the way I walk?"

"Heavy, you walk heavy, you would literally never…" He

rolled to his side, abs on display. "…and I do mean never, be able to sneak up on someone, you're all heel no toe."

"Well, you're a… you're a—"

He grinned and cupped his ear, his messy hair chaotically spiking up in all directions. "What? I'm a what? Can't hear you all the way over there."

"THEN SUCK SHIT and suffer from your side!" There were moments in time where you wonder what actually possessed you to just… react, that, apparently was mine as I grabbed my pillow lunged toward his bed, then managed to launch my body on top of his and just push.

I shoved the pillow over his face and wrapped my arms around his neck.

He flailed a bit, like a fish, a very sad dying goldfish that you'd never remember at the end of the day. But when I started to pull back, he flipped me against the wall and said words I would never forget. "I'm glad you like it rough. You've been getting soft lately."

His hand reached to my hips and squeezed.

I gripped him by the hair and tugged. "Touch me again like that and I'm going to cut off your balls in the middle of the night!"

He grinned. "Aw, baby girl, would that be the first time you touched a man? I think I'd actually be impressed with your bravery." He lifted his hand. "Up top, let's high five over this adventure."

"AGHHHHHH!" I didn't think my scream would actually cause knocking on the door or that in a panic I'd dive under his covers and just lay there limp, like the goldfish I just imagined him being, but when the door suddenly burst open, it was a voice I did not want to hear.

"Typical." Ash sighed. "So typical. And I can see you by the way, also we've been monitoring you guys for twenty-four hours and this is how well you've gotten along?"

Junior's voice was next. "I hate siblings."

"Hey, back up." Ash groaned. "We're all in this together."

"Like High School Musical." Junior agreed. "Wait, am I Troy then, or are you?"

"You do have the better voice." Ash let out a long sigh. "Damn it, should have taken voice lessons instead of working my ass off in the gym and beating you up, regrets always come later in life, you know?"

"Word."

Ivan groaned next to me. "Let us die in peace."

"Classes…" Ash clapped his hands three times before he continued speaking. "…start tomorrow, get your shit together or you really will be dead."

Junior coughed out a "He, like literally, killed one of his cousins, so… I'm just going to leave on those very encouraging parting words."

"Asshole." Ash growled. "It was a direct order."

"Blood… must be spilled." Junior agreed. "Oh, and that includes you two, don't think we'll give you a soft pass just because you're Family, even you, Bella. You have one job, don't be assholes. We're trying to keep you alive, but you will be dead if you don't get with the program."

CHAPTER Seven

Pretend to give up and you just might...
—King Campisi

Ivan

I wasn't quite sure how long we lay there after the stomping down the hall stopped, you know, paired with students fainting in the hall. At least that's how I imagined it, like they were some sort of mafia Elvises.

Shit, what a psychotic pair.

Bella was still next to me, the blanket half on my, er… um, half-naked body. I mean, I had on black tight briefs, so the size of the lower half of my body didn't traumatize her—even in the dark, but that was it.

And being a guy kind of went like this: Oh look, legs. Huh, boobs, a waist, look hands, nose, oh damn it, mouth, soft, hateful, puffy wet little mouth, and then the final downfall…

A stunningly, sickeningly, beautiful pink tongue. What was it about her pink tongue that set me on fire? I was pissed as I stared at the way she licked at her lips, the same way she was pissed at the way I'd randomly pinched her on the hips with my fingertips. She burned to murder me in those moments and my fingers burned to do it again just to see how far I could push her, feeling anything while you were in the mafia and as young as we both were—sometimes meant everything.

Still lost in my little fantasy of annoying her, a sharp elbow came at me right near my spleen, sending me coughing to the other side of the bed while taking the covers with me. "Why?"

"Because you're breathing," she hissed and stomped back over to her side, why was she walking so loud? What was the point? To torture the people on the floor below us or to prove something to me, like the fact that she knew how to use every part of her body, including her feet, to torture other people? I stretched my arms high then glanced over my right shoulder, she was still in short shorts and a tank top as if I wouldn't stare even if she was the devil. Hello, college guy, all I thought was ass and thighs, I was in no position to think about her poisoned heart and lack of soul.

"You know…" I grinned, crossing my arms over my naked chest and flopping onto my back, making the mattress springs let out a little squeak of triumph, bet she'd never heard that sound before. "College is the time to experiment and instead of doing that you're just the same old… boring, Abandonato youngest, who hasn't even drawn blood in oh

I don't know, at least a year, have you lost your touch?" I jerked up and gave her a teasing wink. "Or did you just need something to touch because you're such a prude? I think sometimes…" I turned away toward the wall. "…the best path to take is the one not walked or in your case…" I licked my lips and put my hands behind my head again. "Unridden."

God, it felt good to feel the intensity of murder swirling around the thick air of that small dorm room, I could almost taste it.

I waited for her retort, then waited again.

Confused, I slowly turned to my right and threw my body back against the wall when all five foot seven of Bella Abandonato stood in front of me wearing nothing, but a black sports bra and black boy cut briefs that left her ass on perfect display.

She leaned down and smacked me on the cheek hard enough to leave a mark—twice, she really didn't need to do it twice. She glared then, evoking a hundred fantasies about anyone as gorgeous as her, she snapped her red scrunchie against her wrist then wrapped her silky dark hair inside it.

"Oh, Ivan, sweet, baby Ivan, when will you ever learn? Abandonatos, we always finish last." She eyed my dick and shrugged. "Too bad you'll always finish first, and I don't mean that in a 'yay, I won' sort of way because finishing early is never good. I'm gonna go shower now. Get your shit together before I'm forced to get it together for you, we have orientation and I'd hate to make it so you had to limp down the hall."

I opened my mouth to speak when she turned away, only to turn back and shove me against the bed. "Actually, I dream about it, so maybe think twice before insulting me. I can"—the fingertips of her right hand itched up my thigh—"end you with one, little." She snapped. "Second, kind of like how I imagine every wonderful sexual encounter you've ever had begins and ends."

She blew me a kiss and walked out the door, grabbing my damn shower caddy instead of hers—she even took my Yoda towel. How cruel could a woman be? I fell back against my pillow and cursed. "I'm going to kill her."

My body pulsed. "NO!" I shouted and pointed at the lower part of it. "Never! That's the plague where there is no cure, plus, she's from the family that killed them all."

I jumped out of bed and stared at her pink bathrobe and just decided to own it as I grabbed her pink shower caddy and jerked open the door and walked down the hall.

A few girls gasped when they walked out of their rooms, I just pointed the blue loofah at them with my other hand and managed to open my robe. "Don't worry ladies, not everything's a weapon, or is it?"

CHAPTER
Eight

In the mafia, one thing remains true every single time. Insanity turns into normalcy. Your best bet is to accept your fate and just know, eventually you will lose your shit, and it will most likely be in the most epic, down in flames, sort of way. How exciting, so much to look forward to!
—King Campisi

Bella

He was driving me crazy.

And if he didn't stop humming behind me, I was going to suddenly stop and pray he broke his jaw on the back of my head and then tripped. "Pick a different song to hum."

He'd gone from Purple Rain to Baby Got Back, followed by a hilarious, not, rendition of Staying Alive by the Bee Gees.

My ears were tired—I was tired. Try sleeping in the same room as Ivan the Terrible and then get back to me. He didn't snore, he was too pretty for words, too stupid to live (in my opinion), and just the worst hummer in the history of humming.

People would literally give him a trophy to stop making noise.

Hi, I'm people.

"Ivan…" I ground out his name, I sounded half dead, my teeth clenched while my jaw popped. "If you keep humming 'This is the Song that Never Ends,' my fist is going to end up down your throat, I will find something to grab, might be a lung, might be your liver, hell, I might go deeper and grab you by the dick and make it an innie, thus making it impossible to bone anyone but yourself—point is, stop. I know you're doing it on purpose. We both know you can't sing, so I don't know why you think you can hum. I'll admit you're a great shot, even better with a knife. Music, however, is not your calling."

He stopped humming and grinned at me. "I know."

I exhaled. "Thank—"

The humming continued as we walked toward orientation, just like the clenching in my jaw continued while we walked side by side. Why did he have to be the hardest person to get along with in the history of all histories?

His humming stopped when we saw what was on our schedule for day two of orientation, basically day two was just a ton of partying and clubs showing off what they had to offer. But to look involved, we had to go and support our fellow students and not look scary. Oh no, we weren't allowed to look too scary, not that it mattered, they knew exactly who we were. What our Families did. Who owned this prestigious university they attended.

So, whenever we were around the other students, they stared—some were brave enough to talk with us like it didn't matter we had blood on our hands.

I'd started freshman year as the girl to conquer so that felt fun and extremely shameful, but it made it impossible for me to date because I never knew if they wanted me because they genuinely liked me or because of my last name, which in turn made me shy away from any guy.

I'd take it to my grave.

But because of my parents, because of my life—I'd only ever kissed one guy since the bathtub incident, and it was horrible.

I was a virgin.

A miserable virgin who got made fun of by the miserable manwhore next to me for being that way, and every time he commented on it, I felt more and more insecure, which just fed the anger even more.

I dressed like I knew exactly what I was doing on the outside.

On the inside, I could at least admit during weak moments, I was a bit broken on most days, on rare ones, a bit shattered.

I had every reason in the world to be confident, but sadly, money and beauty don't buy you those things. They can't, and if they do, you best believe they're very fleeting and leave you emptier than before.

Ivan could sleep with half the girls on campus, and they'd high five him. He could do a lot as a man, and I wish he understood how unfair the balance was between us. He came from a Family of betrayers and murderers and would get high fives for conquering.

While I was the conquered.

A guy I didn't recognize smiled at me, he had sandy blond hair, was pretty buff, to the point that I would have done a double take if I was even remotely interested, he also looked like he surfed too much or had a tanning package that he needed to definitely tone down on, and was wearing head-to-toe Supreme.

Sigh.

He slowly made his way over to us. "Hey,"

He ignored Ivan.

Ivan hated being ignored.

Like, hated it.

I nodded. "What?"

"Just saying hi." He moved closer.

To my right, Ivan tensed. I didn't have to look to know he was clenching both fists along with his jaw.

"You busy later? Heard a rumor that nobody's been able to conquer the University's queen. Care if I toss my hat into the pot and show you my magic?"

Ew. Did that work on people? Furthermore, baby bird wouldn't be so confident if he knew that I had a knife strapped to my thigh.

I made a disgusted face. "I think even if you threw in every chip you had, you'd still lose based on odds alone, mainly being, I'm not a whore and I'm not for sale and the minute you get any part of your dick close to me, I'm not going to suck it. I'm going to chew it off, spit it out and make you bleed. So sure, make all the bets you want, put in the good ol' college effort, just don't go crying into your trust fund when I make you a eunuch for even dreaming of touching any part of me, okay?"

He paled.

I patted him on the shoulder. "Yup, good talk. Let's go, Ivan."

Ivan smirked and looked back at him and said loudly, "Just try man. By the way, in case you were wondering…" Wait, what was he doing? He wrapped an arm around me and pulled me close. His grip was strong, unbreakable in a way that immediately made me feel safe and seen. "She's already taken, we kind of stay with our own, you know, powerful, rich, untouchable… attractive. Oh, and your fly's been open this entire time, and steroids are illegal, I would know."

The guy started charging toward us. Ivan dropped his hand.

I sighed. Idiot.

"It's always like this, they think they can just power their way into us." Ivan shook his head. "Think he'll go for a right hook first?"

"Mmm…" He was like two feet away. "I think he'll go straight, like a sucker punch."

"Yeah, he's a bitch like that. All right, do you wanna take him or can I just work off some steam first?"

"Be my guest."

"You know, we're always friendlier when we fight."

"It's the blood." I nodded. "Oh, and please, do make him bleed."

"My pleasure, little girl," Ivan said before ducking and then sending an uppercut to the guy's jaw, he went flying backward, as blood spewed from his chin. He collapsed against the grass and grabbed at his mouth, then held up his front tooth. Oh shit, he bit his tongue.

I winced while onlookers cursed and sighed. "That's gonna need stitches."

"His days going down on girls are so done, how sad."

"For him." I snorted. "A celebration for girls everywhere though."

"What!" The guy stood and wobbled. "Gives you the fucking right! I was just talking to her, what? She your girl or something? I'll kill you."

Ivan shrugged. "Yeah, she is."

I had no time to process what was happening before Ivan leaned down and jerked me toward him, then pressed an angry kiss against my lips. His tongue invaded, he invaded, he claimed, he made me his for a too-brief few seconds in front of everyone at orientation, then pulled back and glared at the guy he'd just destroyed and rasped, "Any questions?"

People started muttering under their breaths and quickly became extremely interested in things like the Fencing Club, Choir, and Art Club.

I shoved Ivan away from me and wiped my mouth. "Gross, you didn't have to use tongue!" Imagine where it's been!

Ivan rolled his eyes and used his middle finger to wipe his lips. "Hey, it was a quick save, and he was being a dick. Plus, I've never gotten any complaints about my tongue or anything else."

I started gagging and gripped his shoulder. "Ivan, that's what happens when you pay them."

"Ohhhhhh…" He nodded. "Wow, that's just the thank you I needed, and I don't need to pay for anything, they should be paying me, or at least tipping."

"Ah, so now you're a prostitute."

"Yeah, that turned on me really fast." He sighed. "Let's just get this whole marching around orientation thing done, grab some fliers, be seen and get back to the house, I need to grab more shit anyway."

We both knew the whole point was for normal people around campus to see the popular kids from the mafia acting normal or, in our case, chaotic and then all would be well. They'd report to whoever they needed to report to, oftentimes their parents, that we had a united front, and everyone was happy. "Whatever."

"Have I mentioned your vocabulary, as always, is staggering? One day you'll be able to spell purple, can't wait."

"I was five and the r's were hard, you whore!"

"Shhhh..." Ivan reached for my hand and gripped it. "We're in love, remember? All part of the facade, what a perfect crime novel... but pretty sure most lovers die in the end by way of violence. I think I'd prefer the gunshot to the head than the stab wound."

I shrugged and kept holding his hand, playing my part even though I'd have to wash my own fingers about ten times before eating. My nails dug into his palm, but he didn't even flinch. Girls watched us walk by, eyeing him despite me claiming him. It pissed me off so much that I got even closer to him. It was rude. I didn't want him, but they didn't know that.

I blinked up at him. "You would really prefer a quick death?"

He stopped walking, jerking me against him so hard, I nearly slammed my head against his chin.

Ivan's messy dark hair was tousled from the movement,

causing it to fall across his eyes in a way that had me itching to pull it, but probably not in a friendly way. I gulped and looked up.

His jaw was clenched. "Well, I just figured that it was smarter to get taken out fast, just like my Family, don't you think? I mean, history so often repeats itself, Bella."

There was darkness in his eyes. I'd always told my dad it was there, lurking, and of course, my dad always said I was crazy, that Ivan would never turn on us. But I knew what was in his soul.

If he even had one.

My throat went dry. "Careful Ivan, it's wrong to speak ill of the dead."

"Careful Bella, murder is a crime punishable by law, but I highly doubt your Family really cares. And yeah, I'd choose to go out the way they did, maybe it's the only way I can honor the innocent."

I kicked him in the shin and shoved him away from me with all the force I had. "Take it back!"

"Never." He scoffed, then spit on the ground to prove his point. "You still killed innocents, and that's on your Family's line, that's your karma, not mine. Cleanse a family line? That's bullshit and you know it, do you even know how young my cousin was when he was pulled from his house?"

I wanted to cover my ears. I never asked. I didn't want to know.

Maybe because deep down I knew, the Families will always do what needs to be done to protect their own.

Ivan's nostrils flared. "Fourteen, Bella. He was fourteen."

"He shouldn't have run."

"He shouldn't have fucking died!" Ivan roared, quickly

gaining attention from people around us. "And what fourteen-year-old doesn't run? What fourteen-year-old doesn't still cry! They don't even know how to control their dick, let alone their legs, when someone has a gun! I don't care what sort of Family he grew up in, I don't care that his dad was evil, there is no excuse for killing someone who was too busy picking out his outfit for school and filming it for TikTok just because the blood that ran through his veins was filled with betrayal." He grabbed me by the neck and walked me backward toward the forest by the back fence and slammed me up against it.

My head made a knocking sound as it collided with the tough bark. Blood pumped through my body, adrenaline followed. He wasn't just pissed, he was livid.

He leaned down, and with each inch he got closer, he wrapped more and more hair around his fingers until my scalp burned from the sensation of being pinned on the tree and pulled by his hand. "What makes your blood better than mine?" His green eyes were so unfocused it was hard to breathe. "What makes you think it wouldn't be so easy for me, to snap this pretty neck, to make it look like an accident? What makes you think"—he leaned in until his teeth grazed the skin below my ear—"that I won't love it past the point of obsession, the sound, the feel, the loss of life in my hands, followed by the power? What makes you think you wouldn't feel the same?" He pulled back, my hair slowly fell to my chest from his fingertips. "We're all monsters Bella, all of us, you're an even bigger idiot if you don't believe that your Family is any different than mine. The only difference is some of us own our rage—while others pretend it doesn't exist. But go ahead, smile at mass, shake hands, nod at all the politicians and higher ups, put on some lipstick, and show your ass, I'm sure that will hide everything, maybe even donate some money to the school for those less fortunate, but in the end, you're the one that has to look in the mirror Bella, you're the one that has to come to terms with what you are. Ugly to the core. Just. Like. Me."

My teeth clenched so hard my jaw sounded like it was clicking, it probably looked like I was angry—but I was sad, so sad, that I was afraid that if I took a breath he'd pounce, he'd be able to tell, he always could when it came to me, he always predicted the broken moments and attacked when he could.

The same guy who saved me and kissed me was the same guy who wouldn't think twice about killing me and believed I'd do the same.

The worst part about all of it, I thought as I followed a few feet behind him to the parking lot.

He was right.

He was right.

Shit. He was right.

Monsters, after all, stick together—until it's time to fight.

CHAPTER
Nine

*We rarely see ourselves for who we truly are,
instead we rely on others to tell us what we're afraid to face.
Most ignore that too, until it's too late.
Until, in our work, the blood... tells all.
—King Campisi*

Ivan

I compared the car ride home to the coldest day I'd ever seen in Chicago, where it got down to negative twenty and I wanted to sit on a campfire just so my ass wouldn't fall off.

That was Bella right now.

Her mouth was doing that thing, the thing it did when she was mad and afraid to speak. Sometimes she did, and it came out more as a verbal attack than a conversation, other times like now, she was trying like hell to keep that full mouth closed.

It would be so much easier if she wasn't pretty to look at, I could at least have every single reason to despise her, instead now I felt bad, because I saw the way she was wringing her hands together, the way she was hunched over in the seat. The seatbelt was digging into her neck while she continued to clench her teeth and stare straight ahead.

"Hey." My voice sounded weak, raspy. "I know I'm an asshole, but this would be a perfect time to just punch me or yell, it makes me more uncomfortable when you're quiet."

"I know."

Hell. This girl was her father's daughter. Manipulative to the core. I had to remember that.

I rolled my eyes. "Whatever."

She shrugged like it didn't matter, but I took it like I didn't matter, I always did. I would always be left wanting and she would always be in her tower looking down, no matter what shit I said to her.

I hit the accelerator.

She said nothing.

I pressed it down to the floor, thank fun that someone had swapped out my bike with one of the Maseratis, which they often did if it was supposed to rain, I didn't even have to text them, I'd just go to my normal parking spot and there would either be the motorcycle I drove or a random car from the Family with a man in a black suit standing and reading the newspaper. He'd hand me the keys and walk off.

Literally, it was the dude's only job; he was called 'the guy.'

The guy.

Basically, he was the car guy, the getaway guy, the driver, the one that just appeared and disappeared without a trace. He never spoke, just handed the keys to me and I always said. "Good?"

"Good," was always his response.

In all my years of dealing with him when he got hired, which was at least six, I'd never seen his eyes, and I'd never said more than that one word to him.

Same for him.

Her hands dropped, her right went to the door handle and clung on.

I smirked and stared back at the road. "What's wrong? Too fast?"

"Too slow," she grated out, her voice sounded more hoarse than mine. Had I made her cry?

I shifted and got past one twenty, there was a curve straight ahead, followed by another, it was dangerous. And I thought it. They would miss us, I knew they would, but did it even matter?

What were we living for anymore?

Our only job was to, what? Kill? Be killed? Serve the Family? Sure as hell, nobody was ever going to love me, and really, did love even exist? I saw it in some of the bosses with their kids, with Bella and her dad, I felt it at times with Phoenix… he tried, he really did.

But I had no control.

Over anything.

Maybe I should have been the one that died, instead of my fourteen-year-old cousin. He would have been a better recruit, stronger, for the Abandonato and Nicolasi thrones.

Killing. Killing. Killing.

Money. So much money.

My breaths came out in fast bursts, just like the acceleration, until a soft hand touched my arm. "Now I lay me down to sleep, I pray the Lord, my soul to keep. If I should die before I wake, I pray the Lord, my soul, to take."

It was the only thing I truly remembered my dad saying to me, over and over again, and the Lord, he did take his soul, by way of Nixon and Chase Abandonato's bullets.

I released the accelerator and slowed down and pulled to the side of the road, dust from the gravel flew up around the car.

My heart thudded in an adrenaline kicked rhythm against my chest. Bella's soft fingertips were still pressed against my clenched hand.

She dropped her hand the minute I wanted it to stay a bit longer and whispered, "Sometimes, monsters need to stick together, feel better?"

I nodded. "Maybe."

The sound of rain pelting against the windshield was the only thing I focused on, along with my breathing and hers. We stayed there maybe ten minutes before her phone went off.

I rolled my eyes. "Are you ever going to change your ring tone away from Jack Harlow? It was bad enough when it was Ateez."

"Are you ever going to stop obsessing over Tate McRay?"

"Low blow."

"You wish." She snorted. "Hey, Serena!" She frowned and stared at me in a way that gave me more chills than our almost accident. "No, um, we'll be right there, we got caught in the rain."

I rolled my eyes again. Nice. Both of us, so amazing at lies.

"Yeah." Her face paled. "Yup, totally spaced it, what's his bedtime again?"

Alarm bells rang, not just rang, they clamored in my head like cymbals as nausea washed over me, I vaguely remembered Junior asking me to babysit for date night.

"NO!" I mouthed it. "No! We got in an accident." I sure as hell enunciated every single syllable like a champ. "NO!"

"Yeah, he's right here."

I flipped her off with both thumbs, then both down, then both middle fingers and slammed my hands against the steering wheel like the child we were about to just be watching.

There was no worse hell.

Trust me.

"'Kay," she said weakly. "See you in a few minutes."

I lunged across the consul the minute she hung up. "All you had to do was tell them we were getting arrested, the FBI caught us, you hit a cat, helped a turtle across the road, went into anaphylactic shock over a peanut! It's not that hard, Bella!"

In a rush, I'd unbuckled my seat belt and was almost straddling her.

She smacked me on the cheek. "You're the asshole who agreed to it!"

My jaw dropped because, damn, it actually hurt. I pressed my knee between her thighs and pinned her arms to the seat. "I said sure, as in, sure I'll think about it. He never even gave me a date!"

"You got Juniored!" She tried to lift her legs and fight me, which just meant my knee rubbed between them.

A soft flush lit up her cheeks. That was… interesting. "Is that all I have to do to get you to get quiet? Get you off with my knee?"

"You are crushing me with both your knee and body weight, you shithead!"

Her voice was shaky.

I stared at her mouth. "Fine, just admit my kiss wasn't terrible."

"Your nickname is Ivan the Terrible."

"I thought that was a compliment."

"Do you even read books? Can you even read? At this point, I have my concerns."

I rubbed my knee harder.

She jerked against me. "Stop, seriously."

I stopped immediately and leaned down until I could almost taste her on my mouth. "Maybe one day it will happen, I'll give you all the angry sex you so desperately need, little prude."

She reached between my legs and grabbed my cock. "Or maybe I just give a little tug and baby bird goes flying out of the nest?"

It hurt, but I still had to admit I liked it. "Doesn't feel like this bird is anywhere near a baby, don't make it weird and let me go before you get it confused. All he sees is tits, ass, girl. He doesn't see the trauma of Satan possessing him from behind long eyelashes."

She gasped and released me immediately.

Weird.

I got back into my seat. "So now, *now*, after a shit day, we go home and watch Satan's child."

"Bam-Bam," she mumbled and banged her head against the passenger's side window. "Hey, maybe he's in a good mood today."

I almost told her not to give the universe a chance.

I was right.

Because the first sight we walked up to after opening the door was Bam-Bam sitting in a pull up with chocolate all over his face and hands, bawling… only to have Junior give us a guilty look and whisper in a low voice, "That's not chocolate."

CHAPTER
Ten

Your worst enemy will often become your best friend when both of you are in need of the same thing—sadly, the cease fire rarely lasts. And what often follows is worse than what you accomplished—acknowledgement that maybe the other person isn't as bad as you've perceived, making you question if you're the villain instead.
—King Campisi

Bella

I'd seen love all around me and I was still convinced it didn't exist, and yet exhibit A, a poop covered child and one of the scariest mob bosses known to mankind, mainly because his dad was Phoenix, wiping down a child with a towel, then plopping him in the sink real quick, smiling and laughing, only to get a pull up on him, and hand him off to me just as my sister walked in looking like a stripper—not a cheap one either.

She was clearly ready for date night.

And so was Junior.

He handed off Bam-Bam to me, then made a beeline for her throat with his tongue, waved us off, fumbled with his keys from the counter while she managed to grab her purse and not break a heel, and then they were gone.

No goodbyes.

No instructions.

Gone.

And I was holding a clean toddler who stared at me like he was going to break me and enjoy every second of it.

The door slammed shut.

Ivan cursed and moved slowly toward me. "You think that… um, they're going to make it past the driveway acting like that—well, at least their lust hasn't worn off, probably because they're up all hours of the night with Satan." He walked over and tapped Bam-Bam's nose. "Hi little guy."

"Don't call him Satan!"

Ivan smirked. "I was talking about you, not the baby. He's perfect."

I rolled my eyes. "Then you take him while I make sure there isn't poop anywhere else."

"Suuuurre I can inspect poop, can't I little dude? Plus, it's only him it's not like Ash and Annie came by to drop off—"

"Ash what?" Ash stormed into the house with his one-year-old, a giant diaper bag, a grin, and so many things left unsaid. His hair was tied into a knot on his head, he was wearing a black suit jacket, jeans, and smelled too good to be just stopping by. "Heard Serena was betraying me by going out on a date night so I figured I'd join in, plus now you guys match, each can take a kid, it's perfect. I like clean math, don't you like clean math… Ivan?"

He said this as he handed over the cutest baby ever, that still wore diapers, puked often just because he was learning violence at a young age, and often sneezed out any sort of substance that went into his mouth.

Ivan handed me Bam-Bam so fast my head spun.

Please, and he said he didn't have favorites.

I took Bam-Bam, and he pulled my hair, not the sort of hair pulling I had in mind for date night. I untangled his grubby hands. He was already testing me while Ivan, for the first time in days, looked down at the little one and smiled. "We'll have a good time."

"Keep them alive." Ash slapped Ivan on the back. "We'll grab him around ten, as far as Bam-Bam…" His voice trailed off.

He stared, and Bam-Bam straight-up tilted his head and said, "Thank you."

For no reason.

Only it sounded like "Fuck you" every time.

We were always confused if he just couldn't say his T's or if he truly meant what he said.

Some days, I think he honestly knew the words and meant them.

I shuddered and held him closer while Ash cleared his throat and murmured, "Welcome, little dude, and on that note."

He stalked out of the house.

"Walt." Ivan's tone said it all, like he had already given up now that we were babysitting both kids. "He even looks like a Walt, what the hell kind of Italian name is Walt? Do they really want him to grow up to be an accountant? It's like they spoke nerd over him!" He paused and caught his breath, then used one finger to point at the poor infant and whispered like Walt knew words already. "Walt is not a killer's name."

Walt looked up at him and giggled, he had a full head of jet-black hair and the prettiest blue eyes, one small dimple on his right cheek and lashes that I would kill for. Ivan was right, the guy looked like he wanted to dance in a field of daisies and burst out into song, then knit a sweater just in case someone caught a chill.

Whatever. I wouldn't admit Ivan was right, I think that was part of the rules the Family built for us, don't give in, even if you're wrong, it just starts arguments.

I set Bam-Bam down. "Yes, because that's what you should think when you birth new life into the world… might name him Damon, kind of sounds like Demon, he could kill people."

Ivan held Walt against his chest and pulled down his little burp rag. "It's like being excited that your kid will one day become a sociopath rather than go to college and shed a tear over it."

"Yes." Bam-Bam chose that moment to give me a thumbs up, then run into the wall before falling down, then jumping up and sprinting into the living room. "My thoughts exactly, do you ever just like look at Bam-Bam and think, yeah, he's going to be a drug lord? Because I often think that may be his journey."

Ivan looked around the corner while Bam-Bam stacked his different snacks in a row as if he was getting ready to sell them to the highest bidder. "Guaranteed, if I handed him a chocolate bar that little shit would still only hand over one bag of fruit snacks. A chocolate bar should at least equal three packs."

"NO!" Bam-Bam yelled.

"Shit, he heard me."

"Shit, shit, shit!" Bam-Bam laughed. "Shit, I shit, you shit—"

"—we all shit," Ivan grumbled. "For the record, I'm telling them that you taught him that word."

"He says worse." I shrugged. "All right, let's get them fed and then put on a movie that will more than likely make both of us want to inflict violence on each other."

Ivan sighed and held Walt close to his chest, then put him over his shoulder and started rubbing his back. "Yeah, yeah, I say we order pizza and then feed this little dude some yogurt."

"GURT!" Walt yelled. "GURT!"

The amount of energy it took to even walk over to the fridge was not a good sign for the rest of the night, especially since it wasn't even that late yet. "What's their bedtime again?"

"Now," Ivan groaned. "I think in like two hours."

"Two hours of hell, awesome."

"Well, you live with me, I'm pretty sure you can handle two kids."

I slow clapped. "Wow, you finally compared yourself to a toddler and a baby, I'm so proud that you're seeing what we've known all along. You're a child."

"A child, hmm?" Ivan set Walt in his highchair and clicked him in, then sauntered over to me.

Why? Why was he sauntering?

Why was he staring at my mouth, and why did I feel

the need to grab a spoon or fork or towel—anything to put distance between us. "A child?"

"You said that already. I'll kick you in the balls if you touch me, Ivan, seriously." I tried to move out of the way, but he had me cornered, literally between the fridge and the counter.

Walt was no help at all; he was playing with his hands.

And Bam-Bam was selling fruit snacks to Barbie.

I was all alone with the devil staring me down. It would be so much easier if he wasn't truly one of the most attractive guys I'd ever seen in real life—it would be easier if he wasn't aware how good-looking he was on a regular basis.

When did his white t-shirt suddenly get so tight on his arms? And why were his biceps staring at me like that? Was he flexing? I backed up until my ass was pressed against the counter and gulped. "I'll grab a knife."

"Kinky." He grinned and had the audacity to scrunch up his nose while biting down on his lower lip, sucking it in with that demon-like mouth. Both of his hands moved to either side of my body as he leaned in. "A child? Really?"

"Back off, Ivan." In my head it sounded like a threat, but it came out all wrong, breathless, stupid. God, I hated him. "Seriously." Even my seriously sounded weak.

"Mmm..." He tilted his head and leaned in, his lips touched my right ear while his left hand found my neck.

I didn't shiver.

I mean, I did, but the AC was on, and it was cold in the kitchen.

His thumb rubbed down my neck, testing my pulse. "Do you want me to prove to you that I'm not a child, might make you into a woman finally, someone sure needs to do God's work and pluck that sad little virginal flower."

Hot tears burned the back of my eyes. "Ivan, don't."

I could play his games most days, but whenever he went there, I either got pissed or just hurt all over again. What girl would want a sexy guy like him taunting her, knowing that he's doing it on purpose, knowing that he has the power, knowing that he's somehow taking it from her by making her feel less than for not being a whore?

His mouth touched beneath my ear, just slightly, a faint breath followed. I wanted to push him away, but my hands were still at my sides.

I wanted to strangle him. Kick him.

Maim him?

"Just like I thought… almost… frigid to the touch." He pulled back, still towering over me. "What? No words?"

I clenched my right hand into a fist and slammed it right into his windpipe. "None, and now you don't have any either."

He gasped for air and collapsed against the floor. "How about that yogurt, Walt?"

CHAPTER Eleven

The women in this family are fierce. Sometimes I prefer getting chastised by my dad—and he has a kill list a mile long. My mom however, deals with the devil. Cross her and you'll simply... cease to exist.
—King Campisi

Ivan

I decided the definition of hell was being attracted to Satan's mistress, taunting her only to turn yourself on and then getting throat punched in front of your nephews only to be forced to clean up poop, a green substance that looks like slime but is probably some sort of poison one of the nephews conjured up because they were bored, oh and needing to take a shower because the substance just won't wash off.

The kids were finally asleep.

The parents were nowhere to be found, which meant we'd have to head back to campus in the morning and spend the night with two small ones we had no business being responsible for while also attempting not to kill each other.

Exhausted, I walked into the bathroom and padded across the heated, white-tiled floor. It was my favorite bathroom in the house, they even had a sauna next to it and an outdoor shower.

When Serena had it built, she straight up built the house around the massive bathroom saying it was her sanctuary, which I think pissed off Junior since he saw their bedroom as one, but whatever, I wasn't even going to go there; I didn't need more nightmares than I already had.

I yawned and turned on the rain shower, then dropped my jeans, peeled my shirt over my head and, in true college fashion, shoved the lump of clothes to the side.

Towels.

Shit.

I shuffled over to the shelf of white fluffy towels and jerked one off just as the door to the bathroom opened and clicked shut.

Bella sighed, turned and leaned against the door. "I'm never having kids."

I raised my eyebrows. "Good to know."

"Son of a bitch! Why are you naked?" She covered her eyes.

"Um, because some people don't shower in their clothes, and this is my favorite bathroom. Why are you hiding?"

"Because kids can sense fear, Ivan!" She scissored her fingers open and peeked through, then slammed them shut again. "Put some pants on!"

"No." I waved her off. "I'm going to clean toddler shit off of me, and then I'm going to pour a very strong drink from Junior's whiskey collection, and then I'm going to the basement, where I know he keeps a stash of weed."

She rolled her eyes. "Very mature of you."

I mimicked her words and jumped into the shower. "You should clean up too, don't think I can't smell the applesauce in your hair from here."

"I'm fine." She crossed her arms over her breasts.

Do. Not. Think about breasts while naked. Noted.

I shook the thought from my head.

"I'll wait."

"Save water and stop being a prude, prude. Just hop in. Your bits are of no interest to me."

Liar.

"You're a guy, bits are always interesting," she said, calling me on my dishonesty,

I snorted out. "Not ones that are poison-tipped, thank you."

She started shrugging out of her jeans. Oh, okay, so she was taking me seriously. Before I could swallow my tongue, she was walking naked toward the towels. My eyes locked on her sinfully sexy ass, and I nearly choked on my next breath.

When she turned around, I nearly cracked a molar clenching my teeth so hard. Boobs. Why were her boobs so perky and full? Why did they have to look like that? Why couldn't she have weird nipples? And why did her legs look so long? She wasn't that tall.

SHORT, I lied to myself so I wouldn't focus on legs.

I looked away again and managed to grab body wash while she jumped in and turned the water all the way to cold.

I jumped back. "What the hell?"

She pointed at my dick, and a not-unpleasant hum vibrated through my veins. "Sorry, I just didn't want you to get too excited over a naked woman and you were drooling a bit, so I figured I'd help with the shrinkage."

"Weird, I don't find myself shrinking since this is my normal state."

She tilted her head and stared at my dick harder. "Really?"

I couldn't tell if she really was impressed or if she was disappointed, and it wrecked my pride that I couldn't bring myself to ask.

I gave a dismissive shrug. "Whatever, just clean your parts, Bella."

She stuck out her tongue, but I turned the water to hot again and gave her my back. When I risked a stealthy glance over my shoulder, she had ducked under one of the many shower heads and tilted her head back, allowing water droplets to dance down her chest.

I licked my lips.

I was a guy.

A guy who liked women a lot.

I wasn't immune; she could be the most hateful person on this planet—which she was—and my dick would still salute her and offer to invade.

Damn.

This wasn't good.

I turned away and tried to grab some conditioner.

"Ouch!" Bella dunked her head under the water again. "Stupid soap in my eyes. Ow, ow, owwwww."

I smirked. "Hold on." I walked over and pressed my thumbs to her eyes, "Okay, open just a tiny bit, let the water go in."

She squeezed her eyes shut, then opened them while I helped her rinse them out. I didn't realize I was still cupping her face until she looked up at me. Droplets of water slid down her cheeks.

Fuck me, I'm not that strong.

"Will you punch me if I kiss you right now?"

"Might punch you if you won't, and we talk about this never."

"Yup," I said, as I crushed my mouth against hers. She gasped and wrapped her arms around my neck. I pulled back slightly. "Just... horny."

"College students." She grabbed my hair and jumped into my arms.

"Shit." I mouthed against her as we tumbled back against the wall. My right hand dug into her hip, lifting her leg.

I shouldn't.

It was messed up.

She was a virgin.

I knew she was.

"Let me." I moved my hips against her. No matter how cruel I could be, I knew it was wrong, that I was playing the devil's card, and that I wasn't being the person I should be. But I couldn't stop, and I didn't want to. Deep down, a part of me wanted to claim her; no, not just claim, to stake a claim, to throw a giant middle finger at the other Families and say *yeah, she's mine, and I did this not because I loved your precious princess but because I wanted to tarnish whatever crown she wore.* "Shouldn't it be your enemy anyway?"

She nodded. "Then I'll always remember that the guy who stole my virginity was a complete jackass."

"Agreed." I kept my groan in. What the hell was I turning into?

"Agreed."

Wait, did that mean yes or no?

She broke away from me, stumbling back.

I had to admit, I felt a bit rejected, even though I knew it was my body talking, nothing more, right? "What? Too scared?"

She scoffed. "No, I just, whatever. Judge me all you want, I just need it to be more than shower sex with a horny college guy who hates me and thinks I'm a troll. Call me romantic."

I reached over and grabbed her arm. "Are you willing to admit that you'd never sleep with me because my Family's bloodline is so tainted it hurts to touch me? Because that may just feel like a challenge."

She jerked away, and her lower lip trembled. It was the first time I'd seen even a hint of her wanting to cry. "Is it so wrong, in this world of darkness and terror, to want something for yourself?"

I had nothing.

I stared her down.

Everything about our hatred for each other felt raw, like at any minute one of us was going to suddenly collapse and admit how exhausting it was to genuinely put so much energy into pushing someone away rather than pulling them close.

This time I really wanted to kiss her.

Not because I knew it would feel good or meet any need I had.

I wanted to kiss her because she was honest, she was brutally raw, and she was fucking gorgeous that way. "No.

Sometimes, the right choice is to be selfish. How else can we survive in this sort of world without at least once choosing ourselves rather than the paths given to us?"

"Wow, hot body and wisdom all in one short shower. You know, you could be extremely attractive if you stop being a jackass half the time."

I shrugged. "Too bad it's part of my charm."

"Yeah." She swallowed slowly. "It really is."

I ignored the way she stared at me, and I lashed out, like I always did when people saw too much then got that look in their eyes like we'd somehow shared some common ground or when you could tell they wanted to ask if you were truly okay.

"Anyway…" I shoved her when I walked past. "I'm saying this only because I care, but you really need to work on your kissing skills, I thought you were going to bite my tongue off. Most guys don't like violence like that." I winked, then instantly felt like an ass as I saw the panic in her eyes, like she hadn't had enough time to put her shields back up, so my arrow soared, and it hit flesh. It didn't hit the Bella I was used to sparring with because I'd already pulled down all her defenses.

I couldn't tell if it was a tear that slid down her cheek or remnants of water, but what I could see were her red, swollen lips.

What I could taste was how sweet her mouth was.

What I could feel, I had no business feeling.

I left her alone in the shower, grabbed my towel and stomped out of the bathroom, only to nearly run right into Junior's solid body.

He glared down at me. "Where are the kids?"

"In bed." Why did I suddenly want to say, sir?

Ash popped up behind him, drinking a glass of wine. "They're alive? Cared for? Asses are changed? Swear on your life that you didn't make them cry."

Have I mentioned I sometimes hate this Family?

I sighed and loudly announced, just so Bella could hear, "They're in their rooms sleeping, Bam-Bam was selling his fruit snacks again to Barbie, Walt grabbed a calculator…" Ash cursed under his breath. "…and I'm pretty sure we're getting audited now, it's like he knows things."

"Very funny." Ash gritted his teeth. "He's a badass."

I sighed. "Hate to tell you this, but he's one diaper away from asking for a tie and spectacles." I sidestep him. "But good news, he'll be awesome at cooking the books and won't get shot at. Bam-Bam on the other hand…"

Junior narrowed his eyes. "Are you saying Bam-Bam is too dumb to math?"

You really couldn't win with either of them.

"I'm headed to bed." I pointed down the hall. "I'll find a guest room, crash, then leave in the morning."

Junior yawned. "You can bounce now, just take Bella with you. I know you guys wanted to grab some shit before going back to the dorms. Oh, and you have that party tomorrow night, right? The welcome to Eagle Elite and remember your place while you shit your pants party, God, I miss those days. Lydia said something about stopping by to make sure you guys don't embarrass yourselves with shit music."

I bit my tongue.

Lydia was honestly one of my favorites, but only because she was diabolical and could basically hack any three-letter agency with her eyes closed. She'd never been caught, though her dad, Sergio Abandonato, often had some interesting phone calls with the authorities. Then again, he used to work for one of them, so maybe that's why they don't give him shit.

We all had bets that she'd be recruited before she finished grad school. So far, she was showing no interest, but that was kind of her MO anyway, act bored so nobody notices while taking over the world and then laugh when it goes to shit.

"Trust." I slapped Ash on the back. "If I can take care of your kids with Bella and not end up in prison, I can handle doing the whole welcome to Eagle Elite, try not to shit your pants talk. Plus, last year, I made two guys cry and ended up winning the bet."

Ash rolled his eyes. "Yeah, we'll see."

He walked off, probably in search of his wife and I kept walking, only to get grabbed by Junior and shoved toward the basement. "We need to talk."

Nothing would or could have prepared me for his version of a talk.

An hour later, my hands shook when I crawled into the bed in one of my favorite guest rooms, not even pissed that Bella was already laying in it.

I felt like I was going to throw up.

I could barely swallow.

Hot tears slid in rapid succession down my cheeks as I stared down at my blood-stained hands. It wouldn't wash off; he said it was better that way.

It was better that we had proof.

It was better.

That's all he kept saying when he handed me the knife and made me swear fealty to him. Had the bastard been preparing me for this moment? Was my fucked-up training for this end?

That's what he said when he smiled and choked up blood all over the floor while I hit him.

"Thank you," was how he finished our talk as he collapsed against the ground and whispered, "You swore."

"I won't let you down."

"Good." He coughed. "Time is fleeting, isn't it?"

More tears ran down my cheeks until my body started shaking. He told me too much; he told me things I didn't want to know. He burdened me in one hour with the weight of the world and the Five Families.

And then I did what he asked.

I killed him.

CHAPTER
Twelve

DEATH HAS A WAY OF NUMBING US ALL,
BUT IN DEATH THERE IS ALWAYS RESURRECTION,
AND SOMETIMES THAT RESURRECTION IS THE LAST THING YOU NEED.
—KING CAMPISI

Bella

I was grumpy when I got up. The house was quiet, too quiet, and Ivan was on the ground staring at his hands like he was high or something. Did he really go find some weed?

"Yo!" I threw a pillow at him. "What's wrong? You look like someone died."

I laughed.

He didn't.

His eyes were bloodshot, his hair was a wreck, small

specks of blood littered down his chin. "Do you trust me?"

"Not when it comes to your behavior, no, but if a gun was pointed at our heads, do I think you'd take the bullet for me? When it really came down to it? Yes, I think you would, because you aren't that horrible of a person."

He choked on what sounded like a sob, then turned toward me, his eyes were steely, resolute. He changed in one second, became a completely different person, and stalked over to me. "Do you trust me?"

"You're officially scaring me." I backed up. "Why are you covered in blood?"

"Answer the question."

"Give me a reason why!"

"What if I said your life depended on it? What if I said my life did too? What if everyone's lives depended on this one answer?"

My breaths were too short, I was losing focus, this wasn't the Ivan I knew, the Ivan I knew was a jackass but always joking around in his jackassedness. This Ivan was…

Damaged.

"What did you do?" I asked.

He shook his head. "What was asked of me."

"Was the price high?" Tears burned the back of my eyes.

He let out a shaky exhale. "More than I know how to pay."

"So, you're in debt."

"My life is my debt." He snapped. "Now, do you trust me?"

I don't know why I said it, I don't know why I told him the truth when I knew anytime I ever did he cut me to ribbons, making me bleed emotionally all over the place only to pretend to hold me close just long enough to get what he wanted before tossing me aside, but I ended up saying, "Yes."

"Swear it." Eyes wild, he held out his hand. "Swear it."

I gripped his hand, then wrapped my left hand around the back of his head and pulled his forehead against mine. "I swear it."

I'd lost my mind.

"History…" He gulped. "Always repeats, and sometimes, it's absolutely necessary in order to fix it."

Cryptic.

"I'm sorry." His nostrils flared. "I'm really, really sorry."

"For what?"

He pulled a knife from behind his back and held it to my neck, shoving me ahead of him. "Walk."

"What the hell are you doing?"

"Walk." He kicked me in the back of the legs. I stumbled forward, nearly getting my neck cut. "Walk through the kitchen, say nothing, I'll do the talking, go outside, get into the car, and don't speak."

Mouth dry. I walked, looking from left to right for any sort of weapon I could grab, was he kidnapping me? I mean, we shared the same dorm and holy hell would rain down on him if he as much as touched me.

Did he forget who I was for a second? Did he have an aneurysm?

There was no way he was this stupid.

My dad would literally put a bullet between his eyes and dance on his dead body before lighting it on fire.

I stumbled forward into the busy kitchen.

Bam-Bam was sitting in his highchair with syrup all over his face and Walt had already left for the day.

"Hey." Serena waved at me, her long blonde hair was in a high ponytail swaying back and forth with her quick movements. "Have you seen Junior? He didn't come to bed last night, said he had business and this morning his favorite car's still here, and what the hell, Ivan? Stop messing around. Yes, we get it, you hate her. Put the knife down and eat, you guys have class."

"In three," Ivan whispered in my ear. "Two..." He sighed. "One."

The front door nearly came off its hinges as Ash, King, Maksim, and Valerian walked in.

Wow, even the Russian boss decided to fly in from Seattle, must have been a red-eye.

Ivan saluted them with the knife before putting it back across my throat. "You were almost late."

"What." Ash's voice cracks. "The hell did you do!"

Ivan's laugh was bitter. "What I was told... isn't that how the rules work? A boss tells you to do something and you do it, are you angry that I did it well or that I did it under this roof? Either way, what's done is done, now if you don't mind, I'm going to take Bella back to campus."

"Like hell you are!" Ash roared, his eyes were crazed, they were red like he'd been up all night.

All of the guys looked angry enough to set the house on fire, but beneath that anger was such deep grief that the air felt thick with it.

I thought about the blood on Ivan.

About the questions. And then I very slowly turned my head toward Serena, who was still rolling her eyes like the guys were messing around. My gaze fell to Bam-Bam. Sickness took over; it wrapped itself around my throat so tight that all I could do was whimper.

Maksim took a step toward me.

I shook my head.

His sharp blue eyes darted to Bam-Bam, then back to me, then to Serena. He was doing what he always did when he was in a serious situation. He defaulted to his other personality; he basically didn't feel. Right now he was doing the math, but he would come up with zero every time.

I shook my head again.

He clenched his teeth, eyes cold.

King very slowly walked over to Serena and pulled her against him. "I'm going to need you to be very calm right now. Do you understand?"

It's like she knew the minute he said that, that something was very wrong.

"Bam-Bam is watching your every move," King said tightly. "I need you to take him from the room while we deal with Ivan and your sister and then"—his voice cracked—"I need you to be very strong for me, can you do that, Serena? Can you be the strongest you've ever been in this moment?"

Tears pooled in my sister's blue eyes as he lifted her chin. "Yes."

King pulled her in for a tight hug. "I need you to prepare for the funeral and then I need you to call all of our parents and tell them word for word what I'm about to say."

My knees buckled. Ivan held me back against him.

I hated him so much.

I hated him more than I've ever hated.

Something was very wrong.

Something that would affect me for my entire life.

Something I would never come back from.

My breaths came in short gasps, too short. Ivan moved

his hand from my neck down to my chest and pressed down like he was trying to help me breathe.

I wanted to bat him away, but I had no strength, because I knew that look in King's eyes, I'd seen it before. I knew him; he was my cousin, he was the Capo.

And he had just been dealt a blow that would affect this Family forever.

Sometimes you just know.

I braced myself.

"Serena, please tell your father to come here immediately to make preparations, invite Phoenix, Sergio, Chase, Dante, Tank, Andrei, and my father, then let them know that they will need to bring the med kits. Sergio will need to bring heavy sedation, can you do that?"

"W-why are we needing heavy sedation?"

"Because..." King locked eyes with Ivan over my sister's head... "we're preparing first for a funeral, second—for a war."

"Funeral." She looked around the room.

She did the math I'd already rejected.

The only new boss that wasn't in that room.

Was her husband.

My brother-in-law.

Former boss of the De Lange Family.

"I'm sorry to tell you this way, but Junior is dead." King could barely say the word dead.

I would never forget her scream.

I would never forget the way she covered her own mouth, biting at her fingers to keep the sound in, in front of my nephew, or the murder in her eyes as she looked over at Ivan and said. "You?"

"It is my birthright, after all," Ivan said hoarsely. "Now if you don't mind, I'm going to take your sister back to campus, please let Nixon know that I'll be stealing one more thing from the Abandonato dynasty. Their youngest daughter. I do hope you're willing to cooperate."

At that moment, when I didn't think it could get worse, honking sounded from outside of the house.

At least twenty black sedans pulled up and at least seventy armed men stepped out and stood at attention.

For their new boss.

My brother-in-law's killer.

CHAPTER Thirteen

Sometimes things are lost, and oftentimes people are lost causes.
—King Campisi

Ivan

I walked past them.

They had no choice but to let me. It would be a bloodbath and I'd just taken over the De Lange Family with its own blood.

Junior was the rightful heir to a Family that never tried to save anyone, let alone themselves. Knowing what I knew now.

It finally clicked into place.

Everything.

The secrets, the lies, the desperation, and the need to be

cautious if I was going to actually stay alive and make sure I did the same for Bella in the process.

She would hate me even more for this.

And I knew, as we stepped outside of that house, that I'd left what innocent parts of me I had left with the blood—Junior had played me so perfectly with every moment, the stabbing, the killing, he'd basically groomed me beneath him with this in mind. And he'd told nobody.

I lifted my chin toward Tank—he'd just started working with Junior on making sure the De Lange Family and the rest of the orphans, myself included, were up to par as soldiers within the ranks—just stared at me, face impassive.

"What?" With a shaking hand, I pulled the De Lange ring from my pocket, covered in Junior's blood, and held it in the air and put it on my right hand. "Any questions?"

Tank paled, his eyes flickered to the other bosses standing at the door. "None, sir."

I knew the men were nervous, concerned, but a few of them smirked. I made a mental note which ones and got into the first SUV. "Let's go, Bella."

"You're taking her?" Tank asked.

"You're questioning me?" I laughed. "Of course I am. Why wouldn't I take her? I already stole her virginity and claimed my throne, shouldn't I at least get to keep my prize?"

Tank clenched his fists.

I saluted him with my middle finger. "Relax, she's just an Abandonato, I think I can handle her. Besides, if you ever want to see this pathetic Family rise to their former glory, you're going to need one of the most powerful bosses on your side and they would do absolutely…" I gripped Bella's chin between my thumb and forefinger. "And I do mean absolutely anything, for his cousin, including marry her to the very monster who killed his best friend. After all, isn't that kind of how it happened so many years ago? Phoenix nearly stole her mom from Nixon. or wait, did he just take what wasn't his to take? I get confused, and then Phoenix rose from the ashes, pathetic really, even if he is related, and then the De Langes were weakened, you know why? Fear. You fear what you don't understand and what you can't control. So get this right." I turned and faced the men. "Fear me. Because I have no loyalty and no shits to give. I took this position in cold blood, and I'll kill anyone who stands in my way. Soon, our name won't be whispered like a curse, no, the De Lange name will drop from every mouth with respect, admiration, and fear."

Bella started sobbing silently by my side. She was cracking bit by bit and I knew it was all my doing.

I pulled her against me, then pressed an angry kiss to her mouth, bruising both our lips, making a vow in front of everyone. "As of today, Bella Abandonato and I are engaged as per the rights established by Frank Alfero and Luca Nicolasi, forefathers of the Families, if someone takes innocence, they must join their hands in blood and unite their souls forever to prove their worth and loyalty."

"But—" Bella started talking.

So I kissed her again. The last thing I needed was for her to ask where I found the old rules or who told me about them.

Our teeth clanged while I shoved her against the car and slid my mouth down her ear. "Trust me."

"C-can't."

"Must." I gripped her by the hair and pulled her head back. "Now smile."

"Never." She spat in my face.

I wiped it with a piece of her hair and winked. "I like a little fight."

"I'll kill you in your sleep."

"What makes you think you and I will be sleeping when we're together?"

Some of the men started laughing, I again, took note, and shoved her into the car. Tank immediately got into the driver's seat and buckled up.

We pulled out toward campus.

The party was tonight.

And Ash was right.

We couldn't fail.

Because everything banked on it.

Our very lives.

Now it was all on my shoulders, the fear of slipping up, and most of all, the truth.

Shit, the fan wasn't going to get hit—it was going to burn the world, and I'd bet he'd be the one holding the matches. Had my entire life been foreshadowing this big moment?

We drove in silence. Her hands were shaking in her lap. I reached over and grabbed one of them. She tried to pull away, but I held firm. Bella started relaxing a bit like she knew this was her fate for now, but I knew better, she was plotting, planning.

Tank cleared his throat. "Want to explain, young one, because boss or not, I'm around five seconds away from emptying my entire gun into your pathetic twenty-one-year-old body."

"Glad you asked." I sighed and looked out the window. "It's strange, isn't it?"

"Talk faster?"

"People always talk about phoenix's rising out of the ashes, but they never talk about the eagle who bathes in them."

Tank's green eyes met mine in the rearview mirror, he cursed under his breath and answered back, "That's because where one rises and falls, another takes its place. Eagles are often overlooked, they bathe themselves in the ashes to look like the phoenix that used to be worshipped but it's the same as a wolf in sheep's clothing, they're not there to resurrect… no, the eagle, it's there to destroy."

"And destroy it will." I grinned. "After all, sometimes, there is no choice."

Bella looked between us. "Are you guys seriously quoting some weird sort of poetry right now?"

"Settle down." Tank sighed. "It's going to be a long night."

"I'm not sleeping with him!" she yelled, then tried to head butt me.

"Whoa." I shoved her away. "Like I want to touch you."

"YOU DID! You kissed me."

Tank's glare was back in full force. With his nearly shaved head and angry eyes, I almost felt the need to sink into my seat for a second.

I held up my hands. "It was an accident!"

"WE WERE NAKED IN A SHOWER AND IT WAS AN ACCIDENT? JUST LIKE YOU KILLING JUNIOR? WHAT DID YOU SLIP ON YOUR OTHER GUN?"

I looked to Tank for help.

He held up his hands and turned up the music like he was already finished before we began.

Yeah, it was my war now, and I'd basically just captured Helen of Troy without permission. My demise would be swift if Nixon caught me, which is why I needed proof.

Damn.

There was no rule book for rage and retribution, for destruction and war.

When we pulled up to campus word, I assumed word had already spread if the general fear in people's faces was to be believed.

I hopped out of the car and pulled Bella roughly next to me, wrapping my arm around her as we walked toward our dorm.

People whispered, a few of the guys, ones I knew worshipped the ground Junior had walked on, had nothing but anger and clutched fists, good let them think they can scare me.

I winked over at one of the taller guys with bulky muscles; he was a talented basketball player, one of the favorites, Junior had supported him a ton.

He had tears in his eyes.

I jerked my head toward him. He was wearing a blue Nike beanie and black sweats. His mom was Honduran, his dad was from Thailand, so pretty much every girl was obsessed with his smooth skin, smile, and the fact that he somehow managed to pull off almond-colored eyes perfectly, or so the girls said.

He took a step toward me. I released Bella, gently walked up to him and threw a punch right into the middle of his face. His nose cracked as he fell forward.

I rolled my eyes. "Boo."

I sidestepped him and jerked her by the arm, pulling her into the dorm while people scattered away.

I kicked the door open to the stairway and ran up with her lagging behind me, and when we got to our floor, people went into their rooms, slamming their doors.

No security needed to follow me, but I knew they'd be waiting downstairs.

It was this way whenever a new boss took the crown and we wouldn't be here long, they'd move us to a more secure location, but the more people that saw us, the better the ruse of true love and protection, right?

I at least remembered that part when Phoenix was shoving information down my throat over the last few years.

Once we got into our room, I shoved her toward the bed, slammed the door shut, then quickly locked it. "Get ready."

"For…" Bella stared me down, her eyes cold, calculating.

"War." I snapped. "Dress sexy and try to pretend to like me."

"Like hell." She jumped to her feet and charged me, slamming me against the door, my head hit the back of the metal with a thud. Her hands moved to my neck, strangling me. She was strong, but not as strong as me. "I hate you!"

"Do it." I taunted. "Kill me. I won't even fight back."

Her fingers deepened, until I started seeing dark spots, before she jerked away from me and collapsed to the floor at my feet. I slid down the door and stared at her.

She was prettier when she was angry, stunning actually.

I'd vowed never to kiss that mouth out of pleasure, I never thought that I'd end up kissing it to bring her pain.

"Why?" She stared down at her shaking hands. She wasn't a killer, she would never be a killer. I breathed a sigh of relief. Good. That was good, not for my sake, but for her own sanity. Then again… I didn't want to think about what could potentially happen if she actually did defend me or any De Lange, would her father disown her? Would he abide by the archaic rules our forefathers set up all those years ago?

I was told that loyalty came before everything, that blood was law, law was blood, and I was banking on it in order to stay alive.

"Why does anyone who wants power take it, Bella? Junior outlived his purpose, and I took back what's mine, besides, what do you think they prefer? Him? Someone who wouldn't even listen to their demands and was still under Abandonato Family rules? Or me? Someone who doesn't give a shit and is willing to let them run wild and restore what was taken? Your dad, your uncle, both of them helped cleanse the Family lines, they barely left any survivors… children, Bella, children. And you think that's so easy to forgive for some of those men? Knowing that they lost brothers, sisters, wives?"

Bella lifted her head. "Rules are rules, if you sell drugs, rape, murder without reason, look at another man's wife and—"

I held up my hand. "I know the rules, they were basically cut into my skin the minute I was technically saved. Imagine watching everyone you love get slaughtered right in front of you, then moving in with the very monsters who did it. Not exactly the bedtime story your parents told you growing up, was it spoiled little princess? I'm sure you cried yourself to sleep afraid of the monsters lurking outside at night, not realizing they were the very fucking ones tucking you in." I scowled, growing angrier with each word I spoke. "Like I said, get ready, look hot, show some leg, and attempt to wear makeup that doesn't make you look like a pre-teen."

"Embarrassed I'll look too innocent for you?"

"Nobody wants to screw the Sunday school teacher, Bella."

"Oh? Because they want the easy whore?"

"No, because they'll feel too guilty going for it, so yeah, be the whore, because looking too pure is going to make everyone think you're not on my side and I need you to look like you belong exactly there."

"So, by dressing and acting like a whore, I belong next to you, wow, that might be the first real thing you've ever said since that's all you surround yourself with. I can't wait."

I could.

My stomach dropped when I thought about what life would look like for us within the next twenty-four hours. Into the lion's den, make enough noise, and you'll get devoured. And we were about to go out screaming at the top of our lungs.

I hope you were right, I hope you were right.

CHAPTER
Fourteen

Revenge trumps love every time.
It's an uncontrollable driving force that leads to nothing
but insanity but once that road is taken, it's rare,
for the person to acknowledge how blinded they are until
either they sacrifice everyone, or they become the sacrifice.
—King Campisi

Bella

I'd never felt so isolated in my entire life. Ivan refused to leave the room. Didn't he have to use the restroom or anything? I spent an hour glaring at him, then crying, followed by looking for one of my knives, only to realize he was already casually searching the room for my weapons and picking them off one by one.

"Here." He tossed one of my daggers onto my bed, the one my dad gave me when I started dating at sixteen, the one he said to use without asking questions first. It bounced next to my thigh. "You can use that tonight."

"To carve off your pretty hair?"

Ivan grinned and peeled his shirt over his muscular body and tossed it onto his bed. "Aw, you like my hair?"

"It's really your only strength since your personality matches up with the devil, so sure, your hair's fine."

My phone started buzzing.

He stared at it… then back up at me, his green eyes cruel. "Aren't you going to answer Daddy?"

Throat dry, I shakily reached for my phone.

"Put it on speakerphone," he barked as he walked over to me, then knelt at my feet and waited, his eyes not blinking. "Now."

I cleared my throat and answered on the third ring. "Hi Dad."

"Hi Dad?" he roared. "HI DAD?"

I squeezed my eyes shut to keep the tears in. "Sorry, I'm so sorry, I don't—"

"—Sorry?" he roared even louder, breaking my heart into tinier pieces. "Sorry that you picked a side or sorry that you let him screw you!"

I burst into tears and choked out the words. "It's not true!"

"So the video of you two in the show—" He stopped talking. "There was evidence, your mom watched a small clip, it didn't show—" He cursed. "What the hell were you thinking?"

I sniffed. "I'm not an idiot. It's not like I thought he'd kiss me, then murder my brother-in-law!"

"He hates you, Bella! HATES you! And suddenly he wants to kiss you? That's complete bullshit! He's more attracted to his damn reflection than he is to you! That's weak, you were weak, all it took was one moment, do you understand?" I can't believe my dad was saying that to me in that moment, I couldn't believe that even when I said, hey it's not true… He brought up the kiss and well… I knew I was naked with him but nothing happened. How do you deny such damning evidence? How do you deny that a part of you was weak and did want a moment for yourself? It's not like I thought it would turn into this!

How do you tell your dad that you've never had sex while he's still dealing with the loss of someone who was like a son to him?

He lost his son.

And his daughter was partially to blame. I looked down at Ivan, his gaze was stoic, his posture tense. "Dad, I don't know what's going on, but I'm not safe."

Ivan smirked.

I kept talking. "I'm not safe, do you hear me? He has me and I'm not safe, I need you to send men, I need you to burn the world and take me with you, I can't be by him right now. I can't!"

Dad sighed heavily into the phone. "Bella, rules are rules, you gave yourself to him, to a boss, willingly, and then you left with him, you didn't fight, you didn't call me, you didn't call your mom, you stayed with him, you went back to campus with him, you rode in the car with him." I wanted to scream that I was too shocked, too traumatized, too upset, but I knew how damning it was when he kept saying it out loud. "You chose him," he finally said. "In the end, you know the bosses would have killed for you, would have died themselves."

"So, I sacrificed myself!" I yelled. "I walked!"

"No, you helped start a new war, because you gave in to a fucking twenty-one-year-old piece of shit who should have never touched you in the first place."

Ivan shrugged. "He's not wrong."

"Ivan?" Dad asked.

"Nixon," Ivan said smoothly. "You know you really shouldn't blame your daughter for wanting to come with me, some women just can't resist. I promise I won't touch her again though, after all, business is business. I'll marry her and let her do whatever she wants—you know other than killing or betraying me, and then the Abandonato Family and De Lange Family will have a truce, doesn't that sound nice? No more bloodshed, and your beautiful daughter…" He reached for my face and grazed my lips with his thumb. "…stays perfectly untouched by my sin-stained hands. Isn't that what you want for her?"

"Swear you won't touch her."

"I swear on my life. After the party, I won't touch her again. Ever. You have my word, after all, we need a united front, the last thing you want is for people to see the Five Families start to crack, imagine what depths they would go to. How tempting."

"Why after the party?" Dad asked. "Why are you still having a party, we have a funeral to plan and a broken family to fix because of you!"

"Broken families…" Ivan sighed. "Yes, I have experience with those. Then again, they can't complain since they were all killed in cold blood, or what did you call it? Cleansed, yes, that's right, cleansed." Ivan shuddered. "Such a pretty clean word for something so horrible. It's like you think you have a leg to stand on. I'm the new boss, so unless you want to call a commission before the funeral, this is how it's going to go. You took from me, from all of us, now I'm going to take what's most precious from you—oh wait, sorry—I already took, devoured, licked, and destroyed every shred of innocence, but don't worry, the hard part is over. Now, we just play nice and get along. I'll send you a wedding invite."

He hung up the phone to my dad's screams.

Ivan cupped my face with his smooth hands and leaned in until his mouth was almost touching my lips. "Even your own Family has abandoned you."

"At least I have one." I snapped.

He jerked back and smirked, then rubbed his hands together, his heavy rings clanging together. "I kind of like it when you hurt me."

"That's sick."

"I thought you knew. The De Langes are sick, that's my family line, get used to it. And try to show some leg, your tits aren't impressive enough to get a second look."

Tears burned the back of my eyes. "Yes, because as your fiancé, that's what I want, attention from other men."

"Better than attention from me." He shrugged.

I reached for his hand, then dropped my own in my lap. "Why do you hate me so much? Why are you ruining my life?"

He frowned and got down in front of me, he reached up and cupped my chin. "If you think this is true hate, you're in for a rude awakening, all you need to do is play your part and say I do and then leave the rest to me."

My tears were streaming down my cheeks. "You said to trust you."

"And you were dumb enough to do it."

"Maybe because I'm dumb enough to see past the facade you've always had, maybe because I watch you more than you realize, maybe because I'm hoping I'm right."

Ivan licked his lips and got up, hovering over me, pressing me back against the wall, his knees on either side of my body, digging into the bed. "Shall I prove you to all the ways you're wrong then, starting with helping you get dressed?"

I stared down at his hands and then did a double take. His right hand was shaking, and his left hand was clenched into a fist.

I nodded. "Sure, Ivan, show me."

His eyes flashed before he jerked away from me and went back to his side of the room and peeled off his shirt. "We don't have time for games, plus you'd take more than a few minutes to get ready, prudes always do."

"Whatever you say," I whispered and went over to my closet to find something that would drive him crazy. I finally settled on a red leather mini skirt I'd worn for Halloween one year. Why did I even pack that? I added a matching red top and a long black tuxedo jacket with thigh-high boots. I pulled my hair into a ponytail and channeled my older sister, putting on dark lipstick and makeup that made me look older than I was.

When I was done, I turned around. "Good enough?"

Ivan's eyes started at my toes, and slowly, painfully, inched up my body to my face.

He said nothing, just stomped over to me and shoved me against the wall, his mouth was on mine in seconds. He didn't ask. He just took.

I gasped when he parted my lips with his tongue, flicking

it against mine before he pulled away. "A reward for your efforts, prude."

I reached for my knife from the bed and charged him with it, slamming him against the wall.

He flipped me around so fast that my head spun, pressing my chest against the same wall and the knife in my hand clattered to the ground. "He made you weak. Next time don't make so much noise when you charge me, better you seduce me then stab me, then try to stab me, and get me distracted by this." He slapped me on the ass gave me one last shove and moved away. "Let's go."

CHAPTER
Fifteen

*People often say things aren't what they seem,
but I digress. Sometimes, they are exactly as they seem.
You can't hide the cold hard truth,
especially when it stares up at you with lifeless eyes.*
—King Campisi

King

All of the old bosses were in the room, along with the new ones and every other captain and underboss.

It was crowded.

Everyone was in panic mode.

And everyone was talking at once.

Old bosses wanted to take control of the Families again to keep us safe, in my dad's words, the old Capo Tex. "We're old enough to die, you aren't."

I ignored him.

Nixon was yelling.

Chase was hitting the wall with his hands—punching it and clearly getting upset every time the wall didn't just break.

Ash was sitting next to me like a statue, along with Maksim and Valerian. We were missing one of our own; we were missing Junior.

The men were still guarding the room where we found him lifeless on the floor; they didn't allow even me in and said that his final will was to be buried in a closed casket as to not traumatize his family and friends.

Ask me if I thought it was okay that he'd hand-picked the men to bury him, and I wasn't one of them.

I was pissed and hurt.

I was broken.

The weight of the world crushed my shoulders, I knew I'd have a lifetime of bruises.

"No." I shot to my feet. "Serena, as is her right, will take care of the funeral. Nixon, as pissed as you are, we have to put out one fire first. The De Lange treaty ends in less than six days. You have to agree to his terms for now, once the treaty ends, we'll see if he's for or against us, but the fact that he wants Bella means he wants allegiance. We protect the many, sacrifice the one, do you understand what I'm saying?"

Nixon glared at me and stormed across the room, shoving the desk against me until I was pinned between it and the wall.

I stared straight back.

His steely blue eyes bit into me. "That's my daughter you're talking about."

"And the rest of the Families? What about Junior's son? What about your grieving eldest? Your wife? Your nephews, nieces? What of them, Nixon?" I shoved the desk toward him. "As your Capo, I'm not asking, I'm telling you. Either agree with my decision, or I'll send you off to Florida to sip some martinis and retire on the beach." I slammed my fist into the desk. "Any act of violence toward me or the other bosses, blood or not, will be taken as an immediate threat." I reached for my gun and held it out in front of me, dangling it from my pinky finger. "And will be retaliated and paid for in blood. Are we all understood?"

My dad nodded his head at me first.

The others followed.

Phoenix slid down onto the ground and shook his head. "Impossible."

"Excuse me?" I asked.

He looked out of it, then again, it was his son. He squeezed his eyes shut and turned to me. "I respect your decision, and now I need to make one of my own."

He got up and sighed. "Was there anything else with Junior? Do you know?"

I grit my teeth. I didn't want to answer the question, but I knew I had no choice. "He was branded, freshly branded, on the right shoulder with a phoenix, beneath it; in Latin it read, rise of the De Langes."

"More good news," Maksim said under his breath.

"Shit." Ash rubbed down his face with his hands. "Shit."

"For now…" I ignored the looks of horror on people's faces around me. "…Ivan has men around him, he's on campus, easy to watch, he'll most likely move into one of the De Lange compounds with Bella. He'll want things to look normal, so he'll still go to school with her, then after the marriage, we'll move them into different housing."

Ash let out a snort. "Seriously? A mafia boss just going to chemistry with you?"

"Nixon did it," I said. "Didn't you?"

Nixon's look of anger didn't make me look better. "Yes. I did."

"So, it can be done and has been done." I shrugged. "For now, you know your places. They'll make an appearance at the orientation party tonight with the other cousins, everyone will show a united front while we plan for a funeral followed by…" I shared a look with Nixon. "Elaborate wedding fit for a princess."

Nixon snorted. "I think what he means is, we'll be preparing two funerals, both very real, both very damning, both leaving scars on us all, some more than others."

He stormed out of the room.

Chase and Tex followed, the rest of the guys, Dante, Santino, Sergio, and every other mentor simply left with him.

Leaving us to pick up the pieces, create beauty out of something horrific.

Ash pulled out a chair. "We have no time to mourn."

A tear slid down his cheek before he shoved his fist into his mouth to keep the sounds of crying from filling the air.

Maksim got up and slowly walked over to the door and locked it. We sat in crumpled silence around my desk.

I pulled out a bottle of whiskey. "We have five minutes to mourn, and then we avenge him while protecting Bella the best way we can. Keeping her close to Ivan and watching from afar."

It was more than five minutes.

It was more like fifty minutes of grown men sobbing.

And then, when the tears dried, and the whiskey was gone, all we had was our rage.

CHAPTER Sixteen

*Lying is harder than the truth.
The truth releases you from captivity, freeing you.
Lying binds you and never lets go
once it has its tentacles around your neck.
—King Campisi*

Ivan

We were early for the party, but a few more minutes in that dorm room with her and I would have lost all control. Every ounce I had left.

Red leather. Really?

I thought she'd put on a mini skirt and kitten heels, not dress like a hotter version of Elektra in her slutty popstar era.

I was wearing a black tuxedo jacket with silver and a vest beneath it that showed off all my tattoos with matching loose trousers and decided last minute to match her with red combat boots.

I finished the outfit off with four rings on each finger, the De Lange one on my right hand, and decided to go a bit wild and actually keep my studded earrings in both ears.

Normally for school events I was told to dress the part of mob boss, then again Bellas's dad had a friggin' lip ring, so studs?

Probably safe.

Plus, I was the boss now.

My chest squeezed as we walked. I purposefully ran my hands through my hair when we walked by some of the girls on the sidewalk, then wrapped an arm around Bella.

If there was ever a moment to bow down to royalty, this was it, except this walk was different, this was no king claiming his queen.

This was the thief stealing both the crown and everything precious to the other kingdoms.

This was the villain rising up from the fire as it refined his body and daring to claim heaven after a lifetime suffering in Hell.

I'd be lying if I said it didn't feel good.

Right.

I kissed down her neck briefly, then kept walking. "Look infatuated."

"Hate and infatuation are closely related," she said through clenched teeth. "But if you want a show…" I wasn't prepared for her to grab my ass or suddenly throw herself into my arms, wrap her legs around me and start kissing me.

I was caught so off guard that I wasn't paying attention, only focusing on her tongue massaging mine, daring to tempt me to do more, to strip her naked in front of all of her… oh shit.

I stopped kissing her and smiled against her mouth. "What's that?"

Something cold and sharp pressed against my neck.

She grinned at me. "You said to seduce first, I was just following orders."

I chuckled, still holding her in my arms. "I honestly don't know whether to spank you or kiss you right now."

Slowly, she slid down my body and paused.

Yeah, she'd done that.

She'd made me want her so bad that I'd forgotten my role in this, my purpose, all I'd felt was her, all I'd seen was the fire in her eyes, and selfishly all I'd wanted was to capture it for myself.

"Little problem?" She tilted her head.

"Large problem." I shook out my jacket and wrapped it closer around me, then pushed her in front of me. "Walk."

"Must be painful."

"Don't make me strangle you."

"You'd like it."

I held in my groan, just barely. Was I that horrible of a person that she didn't even expect me to grieve Junior? Talk about what happened? She hadn't even asked for an explanation. She just assumed I was the villain in this scenario, her a victim. Hadn't she learned how webs of lies were woven yet? Of deceit?

She laughed. "I bet you like rope too."

"Shit." It was seriously getting hard to walk.

"And I bet if I bent over right now."

I spun her toward me and kissed her again, this time

pressing her against the nearest tree while people watched. My hands were everywhere. I wasn't acting.

I was losing control.

I was supposed to tonight.

And I knew after tonight, I would never touch her again. Was my kiss punishing? Maybe.

But it was punishing to both of us, she would just never know because I'd never tell her. Our kiss felt like my grave, I would either survive this, or I would die while the dirt piled on to me.

That was, after all, the price I would have to pay, the one that was asked of me, the one that was trained into me.

And part of me knew this was the last time I'd be able to convince everyone—and as per my oath to her father, the last time I'd get to actually touch her without losing every ounce of honor I had left.

It was all I had at this point. That one word and the belief that it still existed in my soul, no matter how many people thought otherwise.

Her mouth was swollen when we pulled apart. My men were already near the abandoned warehouse where all the parties on campus were held, and lo-and-behold, the rest of the cousins, the ones who were either at university with us or in grad programs were standing there looking shocked as hell.

Lydia, Sergio's daughter, who was a total riot, slow clapped. "Wow, the killer has a heart, or maybe just a dick? Not sure."

"Crass, Lydia, even for your mouth," Anya, Andrei's daughter, said. She was wicked smart, liked driving everyone around her crazy, she was also one of the top ballerinas in the nation. Everything about her screamed innocence and perfection, ask me how many times Andrei had actually threatened to lock her in her room and throw away the key. She was the epitome of a black widow in a nice, cute white dress with small heels and nude lipstick. Today she was wearing a short white dress and a white cardigan.

I shook my head, he'd trained her well, too well. She was twenty-three and could outsmart almost every guy she met, much to Andrei's amusement.

And then there were Raven and Tempest, Dante's twins. Both graduated from high school after testing out at the age of fourteen, then decided to triple major, so at just eighteen we still consider this their freshman year at Eagle Elite. Both were absolute headaches.

Raven was always smiling like she knew something you didn't; it was extremely unnerving and like she knew everyone's secrets, also unnerving. Her jet-black hair was cut to her chin, and she was currently leaning against the student union building wearing nothing but a short black halter top, low slung ripped jeans and flip-flops.

Clearly, everyone had come out to play the roles they had been given.

Tempest was on her phone wearing a baggy black sweatshirt with no pants, and combat boots showing Ariel, Chase's youngest, something most likely extremely inappropriate.

I pulled Bella closer to my side. "You know your job."

"United front," she repeated under her breath with a forced smile while she bit down on her bottom lip.

I gripped her by the chin with my free hand. "The Abandonatos are in bed with the De Langes, literally, figuratively, and all the rest of your cousins are so thrilled. There is no power struggle, only balance, now do your job and do it well, little mafia princess."

I didn't shove her forward; I didn't need to.

She was meant to sit on the throne.

Years ago, our older cousins—and the rest of the heirs to their Family thrones held one party the first week of school. It used to be invite-only until we started going to school and changed the rules.

It only made sense to welcome everyone so they could see for themselves where we sat and where they watched.

Slowly, Lydia reached for the door.

I was the only guy going to school who people looked at like I was their leader most years. Because of that, they were the idiots. This year, however, I was walking in as a boss.

The metal door creaked open.

Everything was as it should be.

Five blood-red wingback chairs had been placed on a black stage toward the front of the room. Booze lined the walls along with glow-in-the-dark paint. Music pounded through the sound system and the crowd of hundreds of students parted as we walked straight through to the stage.

Bella led the way, and I followed behind her, to show that while boss of the De Lange Family, I was still owned by the Abandonatos; we were still on good terms, and I wasn't leading her anywhere she didn't want to fucking go.

The other girls walked behind me.

Slowly, we walked up the stairs, each of us taking our thrones.

I was in the middle, Bella to my right.

Tempest and Raven sat on the other side of her, while

Lydia sat next to me. Ariel and Anya waited at the bottom of the platform, pouring drinks for the free show.

The music didn't stop, but all of the people in attendance and the ones still waiting outside to get let in did.

Music filled the air, along with the smell of fear.

Rumors ran rampant that we always had a volunteer willing to sacrifice themselves in order to hang out with us, which was ridiculous, but what wasn't ridiculous was what we did every year in order to prove to them why we would always be in power, why this school was so prestigious, and why they would owe all of us favors in the future.

The minute the De Lange Family was brought back into the fold of the Five Families a new tradition rose.

Everyone was of course invited to the party, but not everyone accepted, because to accept your invitation you had to give us a secret for the world to see.

A picture or a video, a confession even, and then you'd be invited to every party for the rest of the year, and you'd earn protection from the Five Families. Some kids were desperate enough to sell their souls, but what would we do with those?

Nah, we knew who these guys were.

They were trust fund babies, spoon-fed by their rich parents, and everyone had something they wanted to protect.

I nodded to the DJ and then stood, holding my hand out to Bella.

She looked up at me, her clear green eyes so captivating my breath caught in my throat.

She leaned up and pressed a gentle kiss to my mouth.

I would have preferred rough.

The gentle kiss was too intimate.

Vulnerable.

And a reminder of what I would never have with her. Ever. What I gave up the minute I said yes to Junior's request.

She ran a hand through my hair and turned toward the crowd. "Lights."

The lights completely shut off, revealing all of the video screens on the walls, videos, pictures, and below them written in glow in the dark paint, the names of all of the people who were confessing.

Everything was recorded previously for us to keep account of.

"I cheated on my boyfriend with my best friend."

"My mom and dad are embezzling money from the city."

"My family is broke."

"My family is involved in a drug trafficking ring."

"I cheated my way to get to Eagle Elite."

"I think I'm a vampire and my parents put me on medicine, but I can't tell anyone because my dad is running for senate."

"I poisoned my professor."

On and on the confessions went, we allowed at least ten minutes of them. Bored, I finally lifted my hand and nodded to the other girls. We all grabbed the red paint cans next to our chairs and walked back down to the corner of the room, some called it haunted, others refused to even look at it.

It was an outline of a fallen De Lange. A relative.

The outline was from the time when the notorious Mil De Lange was killed by her own brother for betrayal, for keeping secrets in order to profit from them—she betrayed Chase Abandonato, Bella's uncle, she betrayed the Five Families with her secrets, which is why it was so important that they were confessed here if you wanted protection and loyalty from us.

The exchange was high—but the power and prestige the

students received was higher, and in the end, it gave us little soldiers around the school doing our bidding, protecting us because they knew in the end we protected them.

Bella walked up to the white outline with the small white candle on the table next to it and grabbed the brush from her paint can and drew an X over the body. "Blood." She swiped.

"In." Lydia followed.

"No," Raven whispered, making another X.

"Out." Tempest finished.

When it was my turn, my hand shook as I grabbed my own brush, knelt down and drew a final X over theirs, as if to represent the Five Families, and made a cross in front of me. "Amen."

Anya and Ariel stepped forward and poured vodka over the floor, then each of them tossed a match into the alcohol.

"Your sins," Anya whispered.

"Are now accepted and forgiven…" She looked up and smiled. "Let's have a great year."

The videos clicked off, and the music started again. We left the paint cans as students started dancing once more.

I still stared down at the outline of her body.

She'd been young.

Stupid.

Greedy.

She was my blood.

And I hated her for it even though I never knew her.

The ending of my story wouldn't be like that, if I went out it wouldn't be because I betrayed the Families or my own.

If I died—when I died.

It would be because I did what she couldn't.

Save them all.

CHAPTER *Seventeen*

I never worry about the past or the future. The present is the most scary because how do you prepare for what you're already going through? You can't. You fucking can't.
—King Campisi

Bella

Four days later

I hated funerals.

I told myself I wouldn't cry—that I needed to be strong for my sister even if that meant all I did was feed Bam-Bam fruit snacks and hold his hand. He didn't understand and kept looking up at me, asking where dad was.

I couldn't get the words out.

I simply looked at him and shook my head, afraid I'd break, afraid I'd cry, and I knew Serena had already done as much as she could.

She was sitting still as a statue in between Phoenix and Bee. Her face was covered with black lace from her hat, but I could still see the fact that she'd already cried off all her makeup.

Every single one of the guys that got up to speak burst into tears. I'd never seen anything like it in my life, some of the toughest men in the world brought to their knees.

Undone.

The church was at capacity, loads of family flew in from Italy, New York, and Seattle. I recognized some of them, but hated making eye contact because it just meant they'd give me a sad smile or tell me that this was Family business.

It wasn't though.

It wasn't fair.

And it sure as hell wasn't fair that Ivan sat still next to me like he wasn't the one who held the knife. Nobody as much as blinked in his direction, people still gave him a head nod of respect.

I wanted to scream so bad—maybe even more than I wanted to cry.

By the time the funeral ended, I was still in the pew while people started to shuffle out to the reception.

I didn't realize that my dad was standing next to me until he knelt down and grabbed Bam-Bam from me. "Bella—"

"Not now." I barely got the words out, choked them out was more like it. "I can't, not now."

"We do need to discuss."

"My brother is dead." My voice was hollow. "So please forgive me for not wanting to talk right now, knowing that the person I'm spending the rest of my life with, according to your archaic rules, is the one who made it happen."

He squeezed his eyes shut and held Bam-Bam closer to his chest. "At least do something with the girls tonight, the wedding is—"

"I know when the wedding is," I whispered. "Is that all?"

"Bella—"

Ivan chose that perfect moment to come back from the bathroom or wherever the hell he had disappeared to.

Had Dad not been holding Bam-Bam. we would have had a brawl. I could see it in the way he stared Ivan down.

But Ivan didn't seem phased at all. He simply smiled at my dad like they were best friends.

The nerve of the guy was truly remarkable.

My dad said nothing, probably because he knew if he did everyone would see that all was not okay with the Five Families. He just walked away, Bam-Bam in his arms.

"Come on." Ivan reached for my shoulder.

I swatted his hand away. "Leave me alone."

His heavy sigh was the only indicator I had before he leaned down and picked me up, tossing me over his shoulder.

I beat at his back for two seconds before just giving up. I hated that I gave up, I hated that I didn't have the energy or strength to even attempt to beat him to death.

I just lay across his shoulder, ass in the air in my body fitting black dress and nude heels, and stared at the ground as he walked.

I counted the tiles.

Five. Six. Seven. Eight.

I counted until I got to thirty; it was getting darker; he opened a door, closed it, then opened another and closed it.

We were in one of the back rooms, a classroom maybe, when he sat me down on my feet again and faced me. "Do it."

"Do what?"

"React."

"To being carried?"

"To death." He grabbed me by the wrist. "React."

I tried shrugging away from him. "Let. Go."

"Never." His sinister smile matched his light eyes in a way that sent chills down my spine. "I'll never let you go, but it's time you let him go. Junior is gone, Bella, so if you need to scream in order to accept that, then scream. If you need to hit me until I bleed, fine, hit me, but you have to react or you're going to be no use to your Family or mine."

I choked out a sob. "You're a monster!"

"I'm a realist," Ivan said quickly. "And right now everyone is watching. You can't mope around, you can't look sad or pissed. You need to look proud that you chose me, and we need to show a united front. Everyone from Italy is here, begging to see a crack in the surface, so whatever the hell you need to do to get your head wrapped around this, do it."

I shook my head. "You know one time I really thought we could get along, maybe even be friends."

"Then you were delusional and pathetic," he whispered.

"What?"

"I didn't whisper it." Ivan crossed his arms. He'd lost his black jacket and was in a black button-down shirt and matching trousers. "Now, get your shit together because later this week you're going to be sitting on a very different throne and I'm going to need your help to make sure it doesn't crack."

"I'd rather die than help you."

"Looks like you don't have a choice in the matter if you want to protect everything you hold dear. The Families will be attacked from the outside and in a day the treaty with the De Langes and the rest of the Families is up, which means if anyone else takes my place, kills me, or sees one of those cracks, they'll try to take over the way I did, but they won't just come for me, they'll come for your Family, they'll come for your cousins' Families, it will be a bloodbath."

"That you started!" I yelled.

He shook his head. "You have no idea what I started."

"Why?" I finally asked the question. "Why did you kill him?"

Ivan's eyes flickered to the ground, then back up at me. "I wanted what he had."

I frowned. "You never wanted to be boss."

"I lied."

"You're lying now!" I punched him across the face, my hand instantly ached. While he touched his own jaw and rubbed it with his thumb. "Why did you do it!"

"Because it felt fucking good to have the power for once in my life," he rasped. "And he was weak, already beaten, bloody, broken, I finished what someone else couldn't. He was weak, and a long time ago he trained me to be strong even if it meant turning my back on blood, yes your precious brother-in-law taught me to fight dirty and I was given the perfect opportunity to take what was owed to me in my Family's blood. I took back our honor, I took back our lives, and I'm taking back the Family—to its rightful spot under a true De Lange willing to sacrifice everything." He leaned down and gripped me by the chin like he always did when he wanted to get close to me and didn't want me biting him or running away. "Now either get it all out now or kneel."

"Kneel?" I snapped. "Why the hell would I kneel?"

He grinned. "I just like seeing you on your knees, it's quite poetic for me."

"You hate poetry and you're a psychopath."

He was quiet, his eyes smiled in a way his mouth didn't. "Thank you."

I kicked him in the ribs then threw another punch across his face, or tried to, he caught my right fist and spun me around, then shoved me against the wall, pinning my arms against myself. "Didn't Daddy teach you better?"

"Yes." I rolled my eyes. "He did." Without thinking, I threw my head back and felt a crack—his, not mine.

He released me instantly, holding his nose. I grabbed the nearest chair and slammed it over his body, sending him into the ground, then stood over him. "I see what you mean, you prefer me on my knees, I prefer you on your back looking up at me knowing that I'll make every day of your life a living hell, for better or for worse, yeah?"

He laughed as blood spewed down his chin. "For better or for worse, and now you feel better, right?"

I refused to admit it.

Instead, I just ignored him and started walking toward the door.

When I got there, he was already behind me; he reached around and grabbed my left hand. "I almost forgot your parting gift…" He slid a blood-red ruby ring onto my left ring finger. It was absolutely hideous, large, gaudy, nothing like I had dreamed of.

Nothing.

It was like the crown, heavy for those who bore it.

I trained to protect myself and my Family.

And now, the only way to do that was to marry the one who had taken everything away from me.

"Beautiful," Ivan whispered in my ear. "I'll see you at the altar in twenty-four hours. Oh, and do make sure you make the rounds this evening, everyone loves a blushing bride."

"I'll never have sex with you," I yelled like a complete idiot.

He laughed, actually laughed out loud. "You think I would ever touch you or be attracted to you? I mean really… think of yourself as a nice little trophy wife, I would never debase you. **Besides,** I promised your dad I wouldn't touch you and though you might hate me, I do keep my promises. He's the type to kill if you don't."

"Then I guess Plan B is to tempt you so much you can't control yourself, then Dad can do the dirty work."

"You could try, but what would ever possibly make you think that I could be attracted to someone like you?" He left, slamming the door behind him.

"He's wrong," I whispered to myself. "He's wrong."

But the hot tears still slid down my cheeks.

In what universe would I ever want to tempt the killer to find me attractive?

What a desperate, lonely thought.

CHAPTER Eighteen

Life's brightest moments are almost always followed by darkness. But I always believe the darkness manifests so when the light comes again—we let it shine on our face and appreciate it more.
—King Campisi

Ivan

It was protocol.

The men standing next to me represent each of the Five Families: Abandonato, Campisi, Nicolasi, Alfero, Petrov and Sinacore. All that was left was to officially restore the De Lange Family by way of re-signing our treaty, which would make us six, the first time it had ever been done after the Petrov's mixed bloodlines joined the ranks and proved they could hold their own as Russian-Italian. They took a spot that wasn't theirs to take, one that, on this day, I would finally take back. I would do what was demanded of me by way of sacrifice—and not just Bella's or mine, but his.

The church was deathly silent as were the groomsmen next to me, my best man had drawn the short straw—King. I half expected him to just say the hell with it and shove a knife into my back, but instead he looked calm—too calm.

"You high?" I had to finally ask when one of the Sinacore Family elders, whose name escaped me, was ushered into the front row, all I knew was she was from Italy and liked to feed the world and I had no qualms about that, though at this point I imagined she would rather poison me since Bella had always been one of her favorites.

King cursed under his breath. "I wish. No, I'm just a bit stressed out, can't seem to imagine why though."

"Strange," Maksim said behind him. "For what reason would any of us be stressed at a wedding and treat it like a funeral?"

"Curious." Dante grumbled after him. "So very curious."

Ash cursed. "If it wouldn't send the entire empire into absolute chaos, I would slit his throat right now."

King chuckled. "I think that was the tame part of the confession."

"I practiced a better one, but it was too detailed." Ash glared at me.

I grinned back at him. "Thank you?"

He took a step forward; Dante shoved him back. "Behave."

"My. God," Maksim grumbled. "Could he walk any slower?"

"He's ninety." King hissed. "Show some respect."

"Kill me. Straight-up, kill me if I ever walk that slowly, even at sixty." Valerian shook his head. "Seriously."

"I'll do it," Ash said cheerfully.

"Good man." Dante nodded. "Good man."

"And I'm the crazy one," I said under my breath.

They clearly all heard though because every single one of them glared in my direction as if to say, yes, you are and no, we won't ever forgive you.

I didn't show it.

But I felt the loss.

At one point, they'd been mentors—friends.

Now I was the enemy they had to support while plotting my death. I was nothing to them.

I had no parents.

I had no friends.

I didn't even really have my favorite enemy anymore. Couldn't they see or understand, at the very least, how desperate I must have been to say yes to this calling?

Did they ever even really know me to begin with, if they just assume I'd lost my mind this way?

The answer was a resounding no, like a gong going off in my head. I truly was alone in the world and would die the same way.

Nobody would care about my funeral the way they did Juniors.

Nobody would grieve. They'd celebrate, and I'd allow it because in the end you have to sacrifice the few to save the many, if that makes me a monster then monster I'll be.

I'll drink the poison and smile while doing it.

A promise is a promise, after all.

The wedding march began.

I imagined this moment so differently.

I imagined seeing my bride at the end of the aisle, and I stupidly dreamed about it often, it wasn't even about finding true love; it was about finding a family.

Having a family.

Replacing what I'd lost.

Belonging to something that was mine, and that was my choice.

Bella was right. I would never tell her that, but she was right. This was no wedding, this was a funeral.

Hers and mine.

The loss of her dreams of finding a forever.

The loss of mine of finding a family.

It was only loss, no gain.

Every step she took toward me would be stained in both of our blood, every fake smile we gave each other would be our penance. One day, I hoped she'd at least see why, that she'd at least understand that I was sacrificing the last parts of my soul that I had held on to.

Hope died for both of us that night, it was buried right along with our hearts.

The doors opened.

Nixon was in an all-black tuxedo, blue eyes steely, as he stared straight at me.

And Bella.

Was wearing red.

She was a walking sacrifice. In some cultures, it meant good luck, prosperity, happiness, but in the mafia, it meant something else completely.

Atonement.

By wearing red, she was telling everyone around her that

she was part of my sin and part of my atonement, accepting me completely into her family and offering herself up as my equal.

Equally guilty of murder.
Equally guilty of taking over the Family.
Equal.
To.
Me.
My bride wore red.
How very brave.

CHAPTER
Nineteen

You always have a choice. At least that's what people say. But in the end those choices still affect you and everyone around you. So while you always have a choice, sometimes you have to take the worst one.
—King Campisi

Bella

I'd picked out two dresses.

A white one that I'd dreamed about since I was a little girl, knowing my dad would give me away, imagining the look of love on my groom's face and the look of downright grief and pride on my dad's.

I wasn't one of those girls who had a wedding vision book or anything, but what I did have was an obsession with dresses. Every scenario in life could be fixed with the right costume or, in my opinion, armor and dresses were the very best kind. When you think of a dress, you think of something that shows you off. When I think of a dress, I think of something that tells a story for you and helps you find the beginning, middle, and end.

Dresses solve puzzles because they're puzzles in and of themselves, not one is really the same, and they're always drawing the eye.

When I thought about my wedding dress, I wanted something that would bring out the best in me, something that would make the love of my life focus on my eyes and only my eyes.

I went for a chic silk slip dress with a long train; it had nearly invisible ivory straps that went to my lower back, exposing all of it.

It was simple.

Beautiful.

And I didn't want a veil. I didn't want to cover my joy.

The other dress, however, that I dreamed of, was the statement dress, a dress you wore in order to tell a story and make sure everyone knew that you would be the one writing the ending.

It was red.

It had see-through lace across the stomach, chest, and sleeves, was daring, sexy, and it made a statement with its long blood-red train, but most of all, because the sleeves were see-through, you could see my small Abandonato tattoo in black writing down my left arm, it ended right at my wrist, close to my ring finger.

My branding.

My oath.

My life.

I wanted him to see it; I wanted him to see me and know that I wasn't going down without a fight, and I wanted the world to know the sacrifice I was making.

May as well be a blood sacrifice—bathed in an expensive dress.

I sighed and looked at the white one. That was the fantasy.

The red was my reality.

So, I very slowly started to change into my wedding dress, opting for matching red heels.

A knock sounded at the door just as I finished.

My makeup was already flawless, my dark hair was pulled back into a loose braid, and my eyes were alert.

"Come in," I whispered.

When I looked over my shoulder, I was a bit surprised to see my uncle Chase, not my sister, not my dad, not my mom… but my uncle.

"It looks the same." He let himself in. He was wearing an all-white tux with no tie, and if it was even possible, still looked like he was only thirty years old as he walked into the room. It really was impossible to take the men in my family everywhere. Chase was just another example, fully tatted down both arms, up to his neck, captivating smile that held secrets, crystal blue eyes and thick dark brown hair.

They'd make a killing with a mafia calendar. Then again, he was a senator and had the ear of every powerful politician in the world, it seemed.

"Is it time?" I looked around him.

His eyes locked on me before he crooked his finger and then sat down on the floor. "Sit."

"I'm in a dress."

"It's not white." He pointed out. "Just sit."

I carefully sat next to him on the ground, leaning up against the wall by the door. "Comfy."

"Sarcasm from my niece, shocker."

I shrugged. "It's not like I'm ready to pop champagne and celebrate right now."

"A lot of us have been forced to do things we don't want to do, I still deal with my demons, Bella. Sometimes I think if they went away, I'd be bored out of my mind and need more things to wrestle."

I almost laughed. "That sounds mentally sound."

"Hey. now." He wrapped an arm around me and held me close. "Dreams are made to be borne out of nightmares, not the other way around, Bella." He held me tight. "You appreciate the dream when the nightmare is over, but you always wait for the other shoe to drop. I think it's better to experience the darkness first, so you know what it feels like, then to live a perfect dream only to have the rug jerked out from underneath you, leaving you vulnerable without any skill, tools, armor."

"And getting married is my nightmare." I stated flatly.

He laughed. "It wasn't mine, but it should have been, yes, looking back, it was a nightmare masquerading as a perfect dream. Finally, someone loved me, wanted me, needed me, so when the rug was pulled out from underneath me, I was completely wrecked, angry, lost. I didn't know how to deal because I'd blindly existed in that dream, one that didn't exist."

I knew his story. I knew that his first wife was the one who caused the collapse of the De Langes, hadn't I just been at that party days ago hearing confessions because of her? I also know he loved her more than life itself and couldn't pull the trigger. In the end, Phoenix, Junior's dad, took the fall, took the burden out of Chase's hands, and for good reason. "At least you're happily married now, you are living the dream."

"I'm in a tux and have to smile for the next few hours, this is a nightmare and I think we're all out of whiskey. We started early." He winked.

I burst out laughing. Chase always made me laugh. He was the fun uncle, the cool one, but also the one that would quite literally slit someone's throat for looking at me funny. I kind of loved it.

He and my dad had anger issues that only worsened once they had kids. The wives thought it was hilarious, the kids myself included, that were often caught in the crosshairs when attempting to date, didn't find it funny at all.

I smiled. "Remember when you made my prom date shit his pants?"

Chase scowled. "It was food poisoning."

"He hadn't eaten all day."

"So, it was lack of food." Chase shrugged. "He should have eaten."

"You had a machete."

"I was pruning," he said quickly.

"What garden?"

"There was a tree… somewhere."

"Would that be next to the water fountain or the garage?" I elbowed him.

He scowled. "I can't protect you once you walk down that aisle, just like nobody protected me then. You have to take care of yourself and remember why you're doing this. I don't care what went down with Ivan, I don't even care if it's true that you actually fell for him or his tricks. What I do care about is keeping the peace between the Families, keeping us alive, and making sure you stay that way. So, wear your red dress, cry a few tears, and walk like the queen you are. All right?"

"Not a princess anymore?" I joked.

He turned to me and cupped my cheeks with his hands. "Bella, you've always been a queen in my eyes, you just liked to hide it behind a very innocent mask, allowing your older sister to flaunt her crown. It's your turn now. Give him hell."

"I already do."

"Make it hurt," he added.

"Noted."

"That's my girl. Now." He stood and held out his hand. "Let's get you to your dad before he kicks down the door, not realizing it's actually unlocked. He's a nervous wreck, and we've all made bets to see who he hits first."

I made a face. "My bet is Uncle Tex."

"Hmmm…" He nodded. "Everyone else said me or Ash."

"Like father, like son," I said.

His face fell. "Yeah."

I didn't ask if Phoenix was there; I didn't have to, because when the door opened, he was standing right next to my dad, full black matching tux and dark circles under his eyes.

He held out his arm. I clung to it and reached for my dad.

I didn't know that both of them were walking me down the aisle, but it made sense in a gory sort of way.

Junior had been killed by my soon to be husband.

And my soon to be husband was the new boss of the De Lange Family, and once upon a time, Phoenix had held that birthright only to cleanse himself from it the minute he became the Nicolasi boss and was able to escape the darkness of his past.

It was full circle in the worst sort of tragic ways.

The arm of the Five Families that Phoenix so desperately tried to forget was about to thrive under the protection of the Cosa Nostra again, and every time he had to see Ivan, he'd remember how it was achieved.

The wedding march sounded.

Guests were staring at my dress like I'd already created a grave sin. I held my head high.

Phoenix's grip on my left arm tightened. "I approve of the dress."

I smiled through my teeth and whispered, "I won't let the world burn, and if it does, I'll take him down with me."

"Good girl," Dad said from my right. "Be brave."

"Already am." I stared straight ahead at Ivan.

His eyes were locked on me, something that looked like approval glittered behind the green irises and as much as I hated him, he smiled a real smile, like this wasn't the worst day of both of our lives.

I still remembered his angry kiss, his hands all over me, being stuck in the shower with him and wanting more but feeling embarrassed at the same time, and then of course him making fun of me again only to claim me in front of all of the Families like a whore.

God, I was going to die a virgin, wasn't I?

He would never touch me.

I'd be a laughingstock while he slept with other women.

But I'd keep the peace between the Families.

Sacrificing every need and desire I had—for the devil himself.

"Who gives this woman?" the priest asked, standing in all his pure finery, holding his Bible in his hands like he wasn't officiating a wedding in front of murderers. Like he wasn't marrying one off.

Dad cleared his throat. "Her mother and I."

Serena stood as my maid of honor, I chose black and red as my wedding colors and every single one of the girls standing up with her, Lydia, Raven, Tempest, Anya, Arial, and Serena herself had gorgeous black dresses on with veils over their eyes.

Epic. To say the least.

We were mourning, after all.

"And who stands in for the De Lange line?" the priest asked.

The church fell completely silent, still, tense.

This could ruin it all.

"Me." Phoenix snapped. "And my dead son, the former boss of the De Lange Family, bless this marriage. Blood in…" He dropped my arm and seethed at Ivan. "…No out."

"Get in alive," Ivan whispered. "You'll have to get out dead."

Phoenix gave him his back and sat down next to his wife Bee who was looking down at her lap, she was still in mourning too. I didn't blame any of them for feeling this way.

It was time to seal my fate as my dad leaned down and pressed a kiss to my left cheek, then my right and gripped my hand, placing it over Ivan's.

My body trembled as Ivan pulled me against him, nodding to my dad as if he respected him.

Dad didn't move for at least a minute before he finally turned on his heel and joined my mom, who was watching the exchange with worry etched all over her face. I could tell she wanted to jump up and say I object.

But objecting would only lead to more blood.

And enough had already been spilled.

Numb, I stood by Ivan's side, ignoring the fact that he looked like a beautiful predator in his black tux.

The priest spoke.

I barely listened.

My fingers sweat beneath Ivan's hand.

Nobody cried tears of joy over our blessing.

Nobody smiled at me.

I felt like I was going to pass out when we finally got to the vows. I repeated what I was supposed to repeat.

What felt like hours later, the priest said, "You may now kiss your bride."

The part I dreaded.

Ivan leaned in with a cruel smile, his head descended, but he missed my mouth, only pressing a lingering kiss on my cheek as if to start a precedence over the fact that he would never touch me, never find me attractive, never love me.

The kiss was cold.

My heart cracked, but in my defense, I was weak.

I didn't want his kiss, right?

So why did a solitary tear run down my cheek, a tear of embarrassment and loss that even on my wedding day, my own husband didn't claim my mouth, as evil as he was.

It was one more thing he stole.

And it split me into more pieces than I'd like to admit.

CHAPTER
Twenty

*Always bring more wine to a wedding—
it could end up being your funeral.
—King Campisi*

King

"So…" Ash plopped down next to me. He'd already pulled off his black jacket and opened up his shirt, and by the looks of it, was clearly drunk. "How does this happen? We just send them off to the hotel and he—he—"

"Don't finish that sentence," I snapped. "He won't. He swore."

"So, she doesn't even get a wedding night?" Ash slammed his hand on the table between us just as Maksim sat down next to him. "Son of a bitch, that's sick."

Maksim tossed me a bottle of water. "Whose side are you on anyway?"

"Hers," Ash groaned into his hands. "She should at least, I don't know... I shouldn't know, but I know."

"He's drunk?" Valerian mouthed to me.

I nodded.

"She's..." Ash kept talking. "Look, I shouldn't know these things, guys don't talk about these things, but Junior..." He choked out his name. "He told me one time because Serena was pissed about Ivan always giving her shit and was afraid he would take advantage of Bella or some weird shitty shit thing like that, so she asked Bella if he'd tried anything and if she had questions."

"Not really liking this story time," I mumbled under my breath.

"Just listen." Ash waved me off while Maksim and I shared a look. "Anyway, Bella told her the truth, she's never even like been with a dude or a girl. I'm not discriminating or even like, done any of the serious things you do when you're horny, you know?"

I slid my bottle of water toward Ash.

He grabbed it and started chugging.

Maksim sighed. "That's besides the point, that's a good thing, she wasn't running around like the whores we were."

"You were." Ash grunted drunkenly.

Maksim just rolled his eyes while I flashed him my middle finger.

"Anyway, it just sucks, I mean, I don't want him touching her, but it sucks for her, he didn't even kiss her. It's humiliating."

I crossed my arms. "Better to be humiliated than at war."

"Maybe." Valerian didn't seem to agree while he stole Ash's water.

I checked my phone.

"How much longer?" Ash asked.

It was one minute past midnight.

I braced myself for Ivan to come charging toward me. The treaty between the Families was officially over. Either he'd renew it or break it off and all of this would be for nothing.

We needed him to renew it. To keep the peace now that Junior was gone, he was quite literally the only one who could.

And like clockwork, Tank walked up to me with a black folder in his hands. He nodded and set it on the table. When I opened it, it was the contract for the De Lange Family to be reinstated as one of the original Families, and on the bottom was Ivan's signature in blood.

"There may not be any lovemaking tonight…" I slit open my right palm and squeezed my fist over the paper, dropping blood onto his signature. "But at least we have a guarantee of no war. He renewed it. De Langes are officially under my fist as the Capo."

Everyone breathed a sigh of relief.

"And Bella?" Tank asked, taking the folder back.

I felt bad for the guy, he'd wanted to work with us not for them, but we needed eyes on the inside, and he was loyal to a fault, especially for a De Lange.

He was one of my favorite captains.

I thought about it for a minute. "Once they go to the honeymoon suite, send the men away, wait ten minutes, then sedate her if she needs it to sleep. He'll find his fun elsewhere.

I read through the stupid archaic rules that I'm changing this week, from the founding Families. None of our daughters or cousins will have to deal with this ever again, marriage will always be their choice." We'd never abided by the old rules, the fact that Ivan even knew them was alarming, the fact that he called one of the oldest ones forth in order to keep Bella was ridiculous since he wasn't going to touch her, which just meant, he needed the peace as much as we did.

The question was, why?

Why kill Junior in order to achieve it?

Why not let Junior keep doing it?

Nothing lined up.

Nothing made sense.

You didn't just wake up one morning and decide you want to be a boss after years of hating the mafia and fighting for a chance to choose your own major.

I knew something was going on, and I trusted Junior, he wasn't easy to kill, and our last conversation had me wondering if he knew something I didn't.

It was a fucking mess.

Mine to clean up.

Mine to straighten out.

"Call a meeting in a week and Tank, watch the rest of the men. Eyes and ears everywhere. Either Ivan's plotting something…"

Or someone else is.

And has been for a very long time.

CHAPTER
Twenty-One

*Pretending is worse than getting shot at.
I would know. I pretended a very, very long time.
—King Campisi*

Ivan

I signed the contract.

The easiest part was over with.

Now I just had to wait for the complaints from all the men telling me how to do my job and that we should have broken away to prove our strength. Time would tell and I figured it would take possibly a day for news to spread that we would stay under the thumb of the Capo.

Something the De Langes had notoriously hated for years.

Find the mole.

Who was pulling the strings.

Who was barking out orders.

Who had no fear.

It wouldn't take long, I'd only bought so much time though, so I was still nervous. People rarely stayed silent; they were passive aggressive, good with words and good with pulling people to their side, and often driven by their own greed or need for power.

It wasn't Tank. I knew that for sure.

I had no suspicions and hadn't received any intel. I was told to wait for further instructions, and I was told to play my part, which started once King signed. I'd just single-handedly ruined so many plans.

Tank brought the black folder back to me. I opened it, saw blood, and went into a purposeful self-destruct mode.

I grabbed a bottle of whiskey and started chugging, then slammed it onto the ground. "More!"

Tank stared at me, then at the bottle, shook his head, and walked off to get more whiskey.

Sick to my stomach, I pretended not to watch Bella watch me as I got up and joined some of my men at their table.

They were drunk off their asses, possibly high, and had a few women with them who looked like actual prostitutes.

Wonderful.

I grabbed one from Mark, one of my least favorite made men, and pulled her onto my lap. "Where's my wedding present, beautiful?"

Her laugh was so annoying my ears pounded, her long white nails dug into my cheeks as she leaned down and kissed me, all tongue, no finesse, tasting like wine and cigarettes.

I fought not to gag and grabbed her ass. "Mmmmm."

She moved across my lap, creating friction, and my sad dick deflated even more than it already had.

The men around me laughed and cheered.

And with each kiss of this random stranger on my wedding day, in front of every Family, I made a complete ass out of myself.

I made myself look weak.

Easy to control.

Too eager.

Too young.

I grabbed the redhead next to Dio and pulled her onto my other knee. "I really, really like presents."

She bit down on my neck. I forced out a laugh when she was tossed off me and onto the floor by none other than Nixon himself.

"Hey, Dad." I winked.

He punched me across the face, sending me sailing into the floor before picking me up to my feet and punching me again.

It hurt like hell. Was it sick that I liked it more than those kisses?

The pain was real.

The kissing wasn't.

I didn't cover my face when Nixon pulled back for a second punch, but I was saved by a sucker punch to the back of my head by a much smaller hit.

What the hell?

I looked over my shoulder.

Bella was shaking her hand in the air and glaring at me. "Time to go."

I got to my feet and pretended to sway toward her. "I like the way you think." I looked over my shoulder. "See ya, Dad. I'll let you know how it goes when I make your baby girl into a woman."

Hoots went up around my table while I followed Bella out.

Nixon's eyes spoke nothing but murder.

But he knew. I gave him a vow. It was all for show. My entire life was a joke now… and would be until some lucky bastard ended it.

I gave him a slight nod and stumbled out of the reception hall and into the waiting black SUV.

Bella jumped in ahead of me.

There was no crowd. No throwing of rice. No honeymoon.

Just silence as we drove off.

She scooted away from me and wiped at her face.

My heart wouldn't stop hammering against my chest.

Every single time I tried to open my mouth to say something, the only words I could conjure up were "I'm sorry." And I couldn't say them. I wasn't supposed to.

It wasn't part of the plan.

So, I said nothing.

And I listened to her softly cry next to me.

Funeral indeed.

If she had any clue how much I needed her, if she had any clue how much I wanted her in that moment, wanted her to yell at me, to fight me like she always did, to even hold my hand, she'd be stunned.

We all had our parts in this play.

Mine wasn't to play her hero.

And hers wasn't to save me from myself.

It would be a tragic ending.

Queen takes the pawn.

Checkmate.

I checked my phone once we got to the boutique hotel; it was some modern masculine looking penthouse suite that looked over Lake Michigan, and it thankfully had two bedrooms.

Champagne was chilling for us, along with a shit ton of food and changes of clothes.

She was still sitting on the bed ten minutes after I brushed my teeth and had pulled open my shirt and tossed my tie, jacket, and shoes.

I wasn't drunk.

I was barely buzzed.

I was too stressed and needed to be alert.

I could both hear and see her deep breath. Damn, her dress was gorgeous on her. Seductive and sweet, not too sexy, I'd been tempted so many times to run my hands down her arms, to even just brace her shoulders. The sheer number of times I wished she'd trip during our first dance, so I'd have an excuse to touch her more, was embarrassing.

She stood and turned to me. "Can you help me take off my dress?"

Yes. No. My tongue wasn't working, and my mouth wasn't opening, so I just nodded and reached for the top clasp near her neck.

"So, my dad really will kill you if you touch me, hmmm?" she asked.

My fingers froze. "Yes, and he felt the need to repeat it so many times I lost count, why?"

She shrugged. "Then it would be him holding the knife to you, not me. I'd be innocent in all of this."

"I'm not tempted." I lied as I made my way down every button in her dress until my hands grazed right above her ass where her nude thong made itself known.

Shit.

It didn't help that she was wearing a matching strapless corset that accentuated her hips.

"I don't need to tempt you. I just want to strike a bargain."

"Sounds both dangerous and deadly, I'm intrigued." My laugh was dry, just like my mouth. "All done."

She turned and faced me.

I kept my eyes locked on hers. "Well? Is this all part of your plan? Seduce me and get me killed? Have to say, I kind of expected you to be more strategic about it."

Her eyes were swollen from crying. She opened her mouth and closed it, then opened it again, putting her hands on her hips. "You didn't get me a gift."

"I'm sorry?"

"A wedding gift," she said quickly. "All brides get a gift, it's a thing, I looked it up. And I didn't get you one either."

"Okay." Where was she going with this?

A tear slid down her cheek. She quickly swiped it away. "I just think it's only fair that since this isn't a real marriage, since you're going to be screwing everything that walks, that I should get my choice of gift."

"Sounds expensive." I teased, not liking the direction of the conversation. "And I'm not buying you a pony, I remember when your dad bought you Peppermint."

She actually smiled. "It wasn't her fault she had a hearing problem."

I rolled my eyes. "Her ears were fine, and I've never in my life seen a pony escape and break into a person's bedroom."

She smirked.

"Four times," I added. "Methinks she had some help."

"She was curious by nature."

"She ate my clothes and left me a very large gift near the bathroom."

"At least she gave you something?" Bella smiled at me.

And I was taken back.

To the shower.

To the babysitting.

To the constant fights.

Touching.

Sparring.

To my life before the death.

To having a friend I called enemy, and an enemy I called friend. My heart stung with each pound, making its way up to my dry throat. I burned over the loss I created.

I had no idea that I'd look back and miss fighting with her over dinner.

Or that I'd miss my training with Junior.

I'd lost my brother and my best enemy in one day.

"The rules state you can't touch me," she whispered. "But I can touch you. A small technicality. So, even though you're evil, and I hate you, can I touch you, Ivan? Can I make a choice and take something for myself? For once in this mess?"

What did she just say?

I blinked. "W-what?"

"Touch you," she repeated. "It's my wedding night and I'm going to quite literally die a virgin while you die a villain. So, can you just pretend you're mildly attracted to me? Can you pretend for just a few minutes and let me touch you?"

To what end? I wanted to ask. And why did this feel like I was signing up to get tortured?

I tried to turn the tables. "Why would you want to touch me, of all people?"

"You're my husband," she said. "And you said to trust you. Can I? Still? Trust you? Despite all the sins you've committed and will committee? Despite what you've put us both through and the Families?"

I jerked out of my shirt and slowly dropped it to the carpet. "Touch all you want, but I'm not taking what's someone else's."

She frowned. "What?"

"I'm not taking your virginity, Bella."

She actually looked upset about it. What sort of conversation had she had in her head while I was getting ready for bed? Seriously? She should be thankful!

"Fine." She licked her lips. "L-lay on the bed, on your back."

I hid my smile.

Not how I planned on spending my wedding night in sheer torture while a gorgeous woman bossed me around. Welcome to marriage, right?

I lay down on my back and put my hands behind my head. "Like this?"

Her chest rose and fell slowly while her eyes roamed all over me. She crossed her arms. "No, I need you to take off all of your clothes."

I froze. "What?"

"Naked. I want you naked. Now." She actually grabbed her phone and typed something into it. "I'm setting a timer for my gift, give me ten minutes and you can go sleep in your room, I just want ten damn minutes for myself, to forget, can you do that?"

Ten minutes would be a lifetime.

Ten minutes would kill me.

I was already turned on and she hadn't even touched me.

"Yes." My mouth betrayed me. "Yes, I'll give you ten minutes."

"Good. Now strip."

So I did.

CHAPTER
Twenty-Two

When the tables turn, they really turn.
And when your woman asks, you obey or pay the price.
—King Campisi

Bella

It took every last shred of nerve I had to ask.

My pride was already gone, and I decided that queens didn't just get their thrones, no they fought for them, or they took them and the ones who were born into it were destroyed.

So, I would take something for myself.

Especially after seeing his behavior tonight. I was hurt but more pissed than anything because while Ivan was a tease, he would never actually make-out with random women in front of me.

Maybe he forgot all his confessions. He hated it when women smoked, then kissed him, he hated long nails, and he really didn't like it to be too easy for him.

All red flags.

He'd been acting.

It still stung.

But there was more to the story, and I had no more brain power to try to solve the puzzle he kept throwing in front of me.

I just wanted my kiss.

I wanted what was owed to me for my sacrifice—but most of all, I wanted my power and I wanted it to be my choice.

Ivan was powerful beneath me, all golden skin and sinewy muscles spread across his stomach and flexed biceps as he kept his hands to himself. His half-hooded gaze screamed sex, and he wasn't hiding anything from the waist down.

I let myself look my fill.

He was mine. after all, even if he was the worst human being on the planet—he was mine.

"Tell me." I pressed my palms against his chest.

He exhaled a fuck, or maybe it was duck, but I'm pretty sure he wasn't thinking about ducks in that moment. "Yes?"

"What feels good to you?"

He swallowed slowly. "Are you sure you want this?"

I nodded. "Give me something for taking everything, Ivan."

"So, you want my body and soul, is that it?" he rasped.

"I'll take what I can get." I dug my nails into his skin, his muscles flexed—his entire body flexed. "So, how do I touch you?"

"Grab me." He bit down on his lower lip. "Not too hard, not too soft, don't break me, move your hand—"

I was already following instructions perfectly.

"Yup, that works, that's nice."

"Nice?" I gripped him harder; he was stiff as steel, massive. "Are you sweating?"

"No." He shook his head. "Just really hot right now, trying to focus."

"On my hand?"

"Sure, your hand." He opened his eyes. "Now watch me take in the pleasure of your hands on me and do whatever you want."

I looked down at my phone. "A lot can happen in eight minutes."

"It's only been two minutes?" He seemed horrified.

I grinned. "Sorry, I miscounted, it's only been ninety seconds."

If looks could kill, I would be dead on the spot.

"So…" I pretended not to notice. "I just pleasure you, like this…" I moved my hand faster, squeezed harder only to relent just when he looked like he was going to embarrass himself. "Right?"

"Yes?"

"Was that a question?"

"No?"

"Are you okay?"

"No." He took a deep breath. "Are you just going to torture me as your gift or—"

"No." I released him. "But I am going to kiss you, and I know you're not supposed to touch me, but you do owe me a kiss, so you better make it good, husband."

He nodded. "I can do that."

"I have my doubts."

He scoffed. "Really?"

I lay across him, then hooked my heels around his waist and flipped over onto my back, taking him over with me until he was straddling me naked. "Kiss me."

"That's touching you."

"Not really touching; you're keeping your hands to yourself. I only want your mouth."

"Gonna get me killed," he muttered, and then lowered his head, placing both hands on either side of my head.

When his lips grazed mine, I could have sworn a sensory overload went over my body. His lips were soft and greedy at the same time. He moaned into my mouth when I gripped him by the neck and pulled him down harder.

I reminded myself he was a killer at the very same time my brain reminded me he had begged for my trust.

And then I stopped thinking and just… felt.

His head turned to the side as he lifted a hand and dropped it, I draped my arms around his neck and pulled him in tighter. His cock pulsed against my stomach, demanding attention. As his lips ravished my mouth, electrical sensations radiated through my body, settling low in my abdomen, then drifting between my legs, sparking fluttering flames of yearning and want I didn't understand. I moved beneath him, needing more contact. Desperate for it.

"Shit." He panted against my lips. "Forget Nixon, I'm going to die right here."

I didn't have that much more time left.

And I didn't want to be desperate or frantic. Was it too much to just want to be wanted? To want to be loved? And how pitiful that tears were filling my eyes just thinking about it.

Ivan broke away from me and stared down at the phone. "How much time?" I asked.

"Enough." He leaned down until our foreheads pressed against one another. "Do I have your permission? Not your dad's, not anyone else's, do I have *your* permission?"

"Yes." I didn't think about it.

Because nobody had asked me the entire time what I wanted. Nobody cared, or maybe they just saw the bigger picture. It was strange watching the villain ask a hero's question.

It was warm.

It was powerful.

It made me feel like for one brief moment someone saw past the title, the name, past the money—they saw my tears, my grief, joy, pain. For the first time since meeting Ivan, he didn't attack when I was weak.

He embraced me and made me feel strong.

He pulled me up and flipped me around until I was pressed against his lap and moved his fingers down my stomach, sliding my thong away. I jerked when his hand cupped me, his heat mingling with mine until the muscles at my core contracted and bunched, more and more, whatever he could give. Small kisses rained down my jaw and neck as he started to move his fingers.

My breath stalled in my throat.

Then I gasped as my body came alive under his touch.

"Stay with me, Bella." He bit down on the lobe of my ear, his mouth wet, my body following suit. "Just stay with me, enjoy your moment."

Heat flashed over my body, leaving a trail of prickling

tingles in its wake as pressure built between my legs, my muscles tensed. His finger movements became more intense, frenzied… and more focused only on me. It was what I nearly begged for, what I needed-for me.

I forgot everything but chasing the feeling he was giving me, moving myself against his fingers while he sucked on my skin, taking tiny bites, giving tiny kisses until an explosion of pleasure washed over me.

The alarm went off.

The cease fire was over.

A knock sounded at the door, before a key card was scanned, and it opened, revealing Tank.

And a very shocked expression before he cursed, looked away, ran into two walls, and left.

"Think he's going to tell?" I panted.

Ivan rested his chin against my shoulder. "I guess if he does you won't have to worry anymore, I'll be dead by morning." He tightened his arms around me. "On that nice thought." He pressed me down onto my back and lifted my thong back into its semi rightful place and kissed me on the mouth. "Maybe it's better this way."

He got off me, clearly aroused, and pulled the covers over me. "Wait." I grabbed his hand. "Don't go."

"Monsters like the dark." He pointed out. "It's a bit too light in here."

"So, turn off the lights."

"I wasn't talking about the actual light that's bright… I was talking about you." He hesitated, then leaned down and kissed me on the forehead. "Make sure my funeral's pretty and at least pretend to cry."

"Tears of joy?"

"Absolutely, make it embarrassingly epic," he said sadly. "If you hear screaming, you can start celebrating."

Minutes went by before the key card sounded again and Tank was back in my room. "Everything okay in here?"

I pretended to be asleep and nearly choked on my own breath when he walked through the hotel room toward Ivan's room and closed the door.

No gunshots.

No screaming.

No fighting.

I wondered what was worse, the noise or lack of it.

CHAPTER
Twenty-Three

I thrive off weakness of others in a way that scares me, and yet I wouldn't want it any other way.
—King Campisi

Ivan

"I can feel you staring at me, just get it over with." I stared up at the ceiling, huh, never saw my death going this way. Nice hotel.

Gorgeous woman in the other room I wasn't allowed to touch but kind of sort of did.

And blood in my future.

I failed him.

I failed my Family.

"You swore." Tank grated out, stepping away from the door and sitting on the bed, at least he didn't have a weapon out, then again, he probably knew I wouldn't fight him anyway, an oath was an oath.

I sighed. "I also swore to her, and she's my wife and wanted one thing for herself, so I gave it, like a good husband. Nobody asked her what she wanted. I did. I fucking did."

Tank let out a rough exhale. "I know. Any more intel outside of the picture you have?"

"Underground, yes, still pulling strings. The worst has in fact happened, and you're probably on everyone's 'let's go on a killing spree' list, good guys included."

"Yay," he deadpanned. "The picture is still going under diagnostics, we can't see a face, they're wearing a hood and a beanie, the car's blacked out, no traceable plates."

"Right." I bit down on my bottom lip. "And the information that leaked toward Junior massacring Family members and embezzling money?"

Tank snorted out a laugh. "More good news. All traces link to him, if the rest of the bosses found out they'd think he did exactly what she did—betrayed the Five Families but we know he didn't have it in him, not even when death stared him straight in the eyes. He was set up."

"In such a grotesque way."

"Actually..." Tank scratched his face and reached for his phone, then tossed it to me. "...figured you'd want good news?"

I grabbed the phone and sat up. "What am I looking at?"

"Bank records. All of the money was sent to his account, not a penny was withdrawn and then, as of his death, not a cent left."

"But he was dead." I tossed the phone back.

"Exactly. So where did the money go?"

"Not to a corpse," I whispered. "And he wouldn't touch blood money. How much was it?"

"Everything the Five Families promised to the De Langes for staying true to the treaty and it's about to get doubled since you just resigned. They're filling the Family coffers. The only question is who's pulling all the money from them."

I ran my hands through my hair. "Yeah. Keep digging, and I'll keep looking weak, stupid, and easy to manipulate, as power hungry as possible and as much of a monster as I can that makes sense, within reason." I'd also spend the shit out of whatever I could get my hands on just to piss whoever it was off.

Oh, good, well within reason. The more I hated myself, the more I wanted her.

"Don't hurt her," Tank whispered. "I genuinely like her and think she's a good person, it's not her fault she was the easiest target in all of this."

I scoffed. "And me? What about me? I am quite literally bleeding all over the place while also sitting like a giant fat-ass duck ready to get shot for Christmas dinner, shit I'm in the Christmas Carol."

"Does that make me Tiny Tim?"

"Tiny Tank." I laughed.

"I think they prefer ham for Christmas now though, right?" Tank ignored me, as if perplexed over what the main course should be.

I frowned. "Weird. I would say turkey. The Brits like duck, no?"

"Good to know you still have your sense of humor. Try to get some sleep. I have the trusted captains on the outside, tomorrow's going to be hell. I already marked a few of the guys that are taking orders, some of the supplies are missing, it checks out with what happened before."

I sighed. "And is it true? Is he the main target?"

"Them." Tank corrected. "Both of them, from what I've heard whispered."

"Why not take out the Capo?" I asked. "It would cause more damage?"

"Because." Tank sighed. "It's personal."

"How many more will be targeted?"

He was quiet. "All of them."

"All of…" I didn't want to assume. But I knew. It was a repeat, only this time they'd cleanse every single family line, leaving only a few behind to tell the story. It was why Junior was so spooked, why he'd had no time left before the treaty, it forced them to regroup but time still wasn't on my side.

"All." Tank repeated my worst fear. "It's the last thing I could give you before—"

Before it happened. Before Junior died.

"We need to talk to King."

"He's a good actor, but Ash has a temper."

I smiled to myself. "That might play in our favor, especially if Maksim turns it on for us. Yes, let's… start the game and make the first move and see what happens. Oh, and do me a favor and buy a house, a yacht, and a new car."

"Huh?" He glanced over his shoulder, green eyes squinting in confusion. Yeah, I'd be confused too. I didn't need nor want any of those things.

"Make it look like I want the money and power and am going to be drunk off my ass twenty-four seven, easy pickings, in fact, leak some heart condition, that sounds nice. A weak heart brought on by a poor lifestyle…"

"I see why he trained you."

"Because I'm insane?"

"No. Because you're smart and embrace the insanity like a Christmas Goose."

"GOOSE!" I yelled. "Not duck, thank you."

"Any time."

CHAPTER Twenty-Four

It's always the wolf, never the sheep.
—King Campisi

Bella

I hated the kind of sleep where you know you slept but you had scenarios in your head, like a billion of them with different endings so you tossed and turned until you could find comfort only to have voices in your head, more scenarios, more stressors, until you just wanted to drug yourself to sleep.

I thought of Junior.

The wedding, things I should have said.

The funeral, more things I should have said.

And the bedroom, things I should have taken, things I should have done, and finally, things I should have asked him.

Ivan.

In all of this he'd asked me for trust and as many hours as I lay awake and tossed and turned last night, I still couldn't figure out what the endgame was.

I was also a bit stressed once Tank left.

Did he leave Ivan's body?

Why did I care?

Tank was in there for a while, killing was fast, right?

Finally, unable to do anything but stress out, I jumped out of bed, grabbed the fluffy white hotel bathrobe, and made my way over to Ivan's room.

I knocked twice. "Ivan?"

No answer.

Maybe he was sleeping?

Maybe it was a permanent sleep?

And why was I so stressed out about it?

"Ivan?" I called one more time and nothing. I gripped the door handle and slowly clicked open the door. It was completely dark. If I stepped in blood or saw a body part, I was murdering him all over again.

What was I even thinking?

That would be horrible. Truly horrible. I was losing it, maybe going as crazy as Ivan under all the pressure and I'd been married to him less than twenty-four hours.

I shuffled over to the massive bed and slowly peered over, I should have brought my cell so I could see better, but I managed to lean down.

His head was still attached, so that was a good sign, I

didn't smell blood, and nothing looked out of place that I could actually make out.

His face was calm, almost like he had a more peaceful sleep than me, the bastard, his eyes were closed, full lips were pressed together in an almost smirk.

Quiet, I could handle him.

I licked my lips and stared at his neck.

I shouldn't have.

Who had veins in their neck anyway? And why was it more noticeable in the dark?

I scowled when he suddenly snatched my wrist and pulled me against the bed until our faces were inches apart. "Disappointed?"

I didn't even try to shake free from his grasp; he was the sort of guy who liked it more when you fought back, and I was the sort of girl to do exactly that every single time no matter what.

It's probably what made us hate each other to begin with. I was annoyed that he pushed me; he was annoyed he liked it; I was annoyed when he didn't.

I was confusing even myself.

"No." I leaned down until my mouth almost grazed his. "Did you have sweet nightmares?"

"Ahhh..." He didn't touch my face, but he did lean in until his tongue accidentally hit my bottom lip because he was licking his. "I did, there was a woman on top of me, and then she said I couldn't touch her, a monster walked in, and I had nothing but pain instead of pleasure. It was horrible. I might have scars for life."

"Be careful what you wish for." I smirked.

He paused. The air seemed to heat between our mouths

as he gently tugged me onto the bed, careful to pull me to the other side of him. "I wish for a lot of things."

"You can't touch me."

"Did I say I was going to?"

He'd dropped my wrist, but we both knew what touch meant, it wasn't a simple hug or hand hold, it was something much more intimate.

His right hand moved to cup my cheek. "And you? Did you have sweet nightmares or vivid dreams of blood spilled across this expensive floor?"

"Oh, I dreamed of blood, yours specifically."

"That's lovely."

"It was graphic."

"Death mostly is." Ivan grinned. "Does it make you feel better, though? Dreaming of a world without me?"

I hesitated. I wasn't one to hesitate.

He leaned up on his side.

I tried to look away.

He gripped me by the chin. "Isn't it your turn to be so very careful, what you wish for…"

Heart pounding in my chest, I leaned into his touch. His eyes blazed down at me, breath catching, he cursed. "Something's broken in me."

"Because you're a killer?"

"Because I want to punish you for making me want."

"You won't get it."

"Say it again." He hissed. "One more time."

I gulped. "You won't get it; you won't get me."

He gripped me lightly by the hair and turned my head to the side. "One day, you'll think differently." His nose ran down my neck while his wet mouth ran down my skin.

I felt his heated exhale like a drug pumping through my veins.

I gripped the bottom of his briefs.

He bit out a curse.

We broke apart when the sound of footsteps filled the room. I slowly got up and walked over to the adjoining bathroom and shut the door, then slid to the bottom of the floor while whispers were heard from the bedroom.

Hands shaking, I stared down at my palms.

What was happening?

Why was I even entertaining him?

He was more monster than man.

I needed a reminder of what he did, of who he was.

I didn't need long.

A minute later, he slammed something against the door and yelled. "Get ready, we have a family brunch to attend."

Brunch?

They were worse than the dinners.

Everyone was drunk by one in the afternoon by way of bellinis or mimosas.

I groaned into my hands.

"Look good and pure for your perfect little family, Bella, your life and mine might depend on it, oh and if I disappear for a half hour, I'm not dead, but I might wish I were."

That was all he said.

And I was thrust back into reality.

Out of the darkness we shared and into the stark light of truth, my truth, my journey, my purpose.

Smile at brunch.

Tell everyone it was everything I wanted.
Keep the peace.
Mourn my brother-in-law.
Die a virgin.
And look the other way when my husband flirted with the staff.
Couldn't wait.

CHAPTER
Twenty-Five

I prefer war. It's better to look at my enemies face to face than to wonder if they're sitting with me at the dinner table hiding a steak knife to shove into my back.
Less guess work that way.
—King Campisi

Ivan

Every song in the SUV leading up to brunch had to do with sex. It wasn't my imagination and even Tank kept looking in the rearview mirror as if to check on me.

Was I okay?

Absolutely not.

Was I having a ginormous problem keeping myself in check?

Yes.

Was I actually singing Twinkle Twinkle Little Star in order to distract myself from the fresh smell of Bella's perfume or the fact that her innocent little white dress was inching up her tanned thigh?

Hell. Yes.

Why white?

Why was she so tan?

I mean, she was Italian.

And I did tell her to look perfectly untouched, so her dad didn't take one look at her and assume I was touching her or kissing her.

Which just made me want to touch more.

She was the pretty little glass ballerina in a case that only danced when you twisted three times—but you had to find the key first.

And I was the robber, willing to burn down the house in order to find the key, open the box, and listen.

I just wanted to listen.

I was going insane.

Bella cleared her throat and turned to face me, flashing me more thigh. Maybe Nixon knew this would end up killing me more than his knife?

He trained his girls well, I'm sure he had high hopes, death by want.

I did a double take, then frowned. She had a small white horse tattoo on her wrist. It wasn't large, and it matched the one Serena got on her hand a few years back.

Nobody talked about the meaning behind it, and I'd never asked or cared until Junior forced me to get one on my finger, right next to where the ring for the De Lange Family rested—like he knew in advance, the bastard.

"I'm not getting a finger tattoo." I stared him down hoping that I looked intimidating, then again, I was only like eighteen. "Only losers get tattoos on their fingers." I grinned down at his hand. "Oh look, is that fresh ink?"

He swatted my hand away, then flipped me off with the same tatted hand. "You're an idiot."

"Thank you."

"It wasn't a compliment."

"But it kind of felt like one, you know?" I winked.

He smirked and then sobered, as if remembering he was supposed to be teaching me shit. "You'll get the tattoo like everyone else, think of it like a secret club."

I nodded and grabbed the glass of whiskey from his hand and took a sip. "Mmm, a strip club, I could get onboard."

He snatched the whiskey back. "There will be no nudity at this club, no matter how desperately you want to see your first flash of boob, Ivan."

"Please, I've seen boobs."

"And yet I assume you still don't know what to do with them once you've seen them." He teased.

Love/hate, that was our relationship in a nutshell.

Teacher/student.

Enemies/friends.

Take your pick.

"Sometimes..." His expression shifted to something darker, more sinister. "You need to become the very thing you hate in order to beat it. The white horse is an example of what we'll all become. You remember the Trojan Horse? There's meaning there, you infiltrate from within, we've been littered with haunts from the White Horse for years and nobody ever really knew the significance other than it meant death was coming soon, but do you know where it all really started?"

I let out a heavy sigh. "Will I need more alcohol for this?"

"Nah." Junior laughed. "I mean, a story is just a story and I think my dad completely embellishes it at this point."

"So?"

"When his sister, the girl who shall not be named."

"Mil," I said in a bored tone. "Continue."

"Yeah, when she was married to Chase and he almost died, Dad was deep undercover and was still alive, surprise, apparently the mafia likes to pretend to kill people, anyway, he wrote her a note and said that she deserved someone who would leave her favorite white horse under her pillow every night. She'd been obsessed with that stupid thing for years and nobody really thought twice about it until the white horse was used for something other than love. Once she died, it became a symbol of death."

I processed what he was saying, but still didn't get it. "So, it became like the boogie man? A child's toy?"

"Yeah." He shuddered like it was uncomfortable even talking about it. "Anyway, we started getting random stuffed white horses in the mail or figurines and then, for a while, it stopped, during the treaty with the De Langes, it stopped for a while."

"So, what's this have to do with me? It's just a story and not even that scary."

"Killing and bomb threats are always scary, you dumbass." Junior shook his head. "I talked with my dad last night, and apparently they found the original white horse years ago and it was something that he kept in his office to remember the fallen, even though she betrayed everyone."

I nodded. "And?"

"When I went into my dad's office last night, it was missing."

"Maybe he got rid of it?"

Junior shook his head. "He would never. And when I asked him about it, he just shrugged like it wasn't a big deal."

"So, I get the tattoo and it appears?"

"You get the tattoo so you understand that at the end of the day you have loyalty to us and only us no matter what, a reminder that the very finger you put that horse on will get severed if you back down, and a reminder to all of us that the war isn't over, it's quiet on purpose. And, finally..." He stood and grabbed his knife from his pocket and held it to my chin. "A reminder that one day, I might ask you to become it."

"Become what?"

"The white horse."

"Why?"

"So we can finally end it all."

I shook away the memory and mumbled, "Be the horse."

"Huh?" Bella smacked me on the thigh. "Did you just say be the horse?"

"No, I said hung like a horse, same thing."

She rolled her eyes. "Someone's cocky."

"Cock is the first part in that word you know, that right?"

She smiled and then it fell from her face; I hated it. Damn it, I really was the Trojan horse, which just reminded me of a condom, sex, of being cocky, and wanting to punch Junior in the face all over again.

He'd planned so perfectly.

Like father, like son.

Shit.

"I bought a yacht." I suddenly blurted.

Bella slowly craned her neck toward me. "You get seasick."

"That was one time."

"It was enough to make you stop eating shrimp for a solid year."

I made a face. "I just wasn't into shrimp."

"Because you were busy barfing it over the yacht, that's straight up cannibalism right there, feeding the poor shrimp family remnants of their loved ones mixed with stomach acid."

I scowled. "Stop exaggerating and I can own a yacht, we can park it."

"You park cars, you drop an anchor for a yacht."

"I know that."

"Didn't you just learn how to swim two years ago?" She pointed out.

Great conversation. "I can swim just fine."

"Maybe the shrimp ghosts will get you, one can only hope." She smiled sweetly and gripped me by the thigh.

I stared down at her hand; my breathing was too heavy to be normal. I liked her touch; I needed to really not like it. I needed to not like her; I was trying, in that moment, to figure out how I went from constantly wanting to fight with her to needing her.

Was it when everyone abandoned me and saw me as the villain?

No. I didn't care what they thought.

Something flickered in my soul.

"I trust you." She'd sworn.

She was the only person other than Junior to ever say that out loud.

CHAPTER
Twenty-Six

Good liars are too smooth. But honest people stumble over their words because they're afraid you're trying to trap them. Always watch out for pretty sentences formed around compliments—they may be pointing a gun at your head while telling you how much they respect you.
—King Campisi

Bella

We walked up to my dad's house. It was massive, built around our own private lake and had its own golf course that was, of course, closed to the public unless you were invited.

Though, I wouldn't be super thrilled about being invited to my dad's house unless you were prepared to either kiss ass or die.

I glanced over at Ivan as we walked up the pathway to

the back of the house by the pool where mom always set up brunch.

Tons of suits watched us curiously.

Tank walked behind us but other than that, no other protection was needed now that the treaty between all of the Families was renewed, I'm sure it still didn't make Ivan feel any less stressed.

He deserved it though.

That's what I reminded myself as I held his hand and kept my head high. He deserved what was coming to him because he was the one in the end that made that choice.

It was idyllic, really.

Brunch was set around the table, small little cucumber sandwiches, four large carafes of mimosas, more wine as per usual, eggs, bacon, sausage, hummus, bread, and cheese boards.

They went all out the day after selling me to the devil.

My heart clenched in my chest, no matter what did or didn't happen, I still wanted my dad to look at me like he was proud, but he was expressionless. I wanted to run into his arms and cry. I wanted my mom to tell me it was going to be okay, instead she tucked her dark hair behind her ears and whispered something to my dad then gave him a shove.

He pushed his metal chair back and stood; he was wearing baby blue jeans and a white button-down shirt, clearly unbuttoned two buttons to show off the Abandonato Family crest and the three jagged knife scars across the ink.

Ivan, to his credit, didn't back away; he simply stared Dad down and then held out his hand.

His hand lingered in the space between them. Awkward did not even begin to cover it.

Dad stared it down, then looked up at Ivan. "Did you touch her?"

"You told me not to." Ivan tilted his head. "Have the rules changed?"

Dad's eyes narrowed. "You're married to her in name only, that was the deal."

Ivan jerked me against his side. "Trust me, the last thing she wants is me actually touching her. I'm tainted, my entire family line is, right? Why would I expect you to change your mind, even if that means your precious daughter is happy?"

I tried to pull away, but he wouldn't let me.

"Yeah." Dad eyed me up and down. "She looks thrilled."

"Whose fault is that?" Ivan snapped.

"Yours. Hers. Hormones. Old laws I'll sure as hell be fighting to fix as soon as humanly possible." Dad gritted his teeth. "Take your pick, and take a seat, we're still waiting on Ash and King. The others ate."

Oh, no. So, my overprotective cousin who was quick to anger, and the cousin who's the new Capo and likes to feed his rage.

That doesn't sound like a brunch disaster.

Maybe they'd bring their wives.

Mom eyed me from the end of the table, her brown eyes narrowed between us, and then a small smirk formed on her lips. "If you'll excuse me."

"No!" I shouted.

Mom grinned. "Yeah, I think I forgot my mimosa inside, you can join me if you want?"

Thank God.

I bolted after her, clinging to her like she was my lifeline as we made our way inside the kitchen, it was like we could finally breathe.

"Go on." She handed me a glass and then added a heavy pour of champagne into the glass with a drop of orange juice. "Drink, your dad's still angry, mostly at himself for the loophole Ivan more than cheerfully jumped through, though I think he would have tried to take you regardless."

I rolled my eyes and leaned my hip against the counter, staring outside at the huge breakfast table, the fountain behind it in the pool, and the green leading out to the golf course. "No, he never wanted me, he never will. So, cheers to a loveless arranged marriage with a killer, we do have more champagne, right?"

Mom grabbed her glass and joined me against the counter. She looked so refined in her white pantsuit, with her matching vest and gold jewelry. "Hate and love are very fine lines that most idiots tend to play with, take a look at your dad."

I snorted into my drink.

She shrugged. "Shall we call him exhibit A?"

"Mommmm, he loved you since he was a teenager. I've heard the story a million times."

"Your dad was a complete asshole, ask Uncle Chase."

I scrunched up my nose. "Don't need to hear that sordid love triangle story ever again, my ears still bleed."

She took a small sip. "Chase will always be one of our best friends, it was a phase brought on by pain, and your dad, well, still an ass."

"Cheers." I clinked my glass against hers.

"So…" Mom's voice changed to the serious voice, the one moms get when they're ready to say something like, *I have to talk to you about something*. "Did he?"

I finished my mimosa and reached for the champagne bottle. "What?"

"Touch you? Break the rules?"

I was always honest with my mom; I could literally tell her that I had a body in the back of my car, and she'd just grab my keys and ask me to bring something flammable while searching for matches.

"Nobody asked me"—I sighed, taking another drink from the cold glass.—"what I wanted, he did."

Mom's eyebrows rose. "Oh? And what was your answer?"

My cheeks burned red-hot; I could feel the flush. "I told him I wanted ten minutes, and I begged him to break the rules."

"And did he? Break the rules for you?"

"I'm still a virgin, regardless of what you both think, I'll probably die that way." I set my glass down. "But yeah, he did touch me, he touched me because I wanted something for me on my wedding night, something that was taken from me."

Mom wrapped an arm around me and pulled me in close. She smelled like Dior perfume and was so warm. "It's going to work out, you know before all of this, I thought he had a crush on you."

I laughed. "Yeah, that's why we had laminated the rules and made copies for everyone's houses, because we had crushes."

Mom kissed me on the forehead. "This family is strange, but we like to fight and fighting more often than not means something else entirely. Think of it as our love language."

"Wow." I laughed. "Healthy."

She pointed her glass at me. "I didn't say it was healthy, or that we were mentally stable."

The sound of fighting broke out from the outside. I didn't waste any time and ran out just in time to see Ash throw a punch across Ivan's face.

Seriously? Already?

Ivan crumpled to the ground.

Why wasn't he fighting back?

"Fucking Trojan Horse." Ivan rubbed his jaw as blood dripped down his chin. "You could have broken a molar!"

"Trojan Horse?" Ash repeated.

Phoenix was standing next to Dad, eyes pensive. "What did he say again?"

"Trojan, like the condoms I used on your daughter last night." Ivan winked over at me. "Right? I mean, we may as well—"

King kicked him in the ribs. "You swore."

"I was joking!"

"It's not fucking funny!" Ash roared, pulling him to his feet. "We'll be back, don't wait for us."

They took him away just like that.

And my dad let them, just like that.

He sat with Phoenix and ate biscuits and jam while my mom grabbed more champagne and joined in on the conversation like Ivan wasn't probably getting the crap beat out of him; I was pissed because he used me every time and he wasn't even being honest!

For every moment he gave me that was tender, he ripped another away with crassness and with his words.

It was like last night never even happened.

With one cheap phrase.

He stole that from me too.

And now I was empty again.

Staring out at a golf course, I wanted to burn to the ground, listening to my family laugh, watching kids play, and feeling sorry for myself, wondering why everyone in this godforsaken Family had something or someone to love.

And I had…

Nothing.

CHAPTER Twenty-Seven

What a lie, what an epic lie.
—King Campisi

Ivan

"I said to hit me in the text and get me away from Phoenix and Nixon, not to like actually draw blood, you jackass!" I roared, throwing the bloody rag at Ash's face.

He popped his knuckles and leaned over in his steel chair. "Sorry, it was just burning to get out, may have overdone it."

My mouth filled with blood. "You think?"

I spat onto the ground.

King smirked from his spot in the mother-in-law suite, he grabbed an ice pack. "Now, tell us how you know the phrase and the meaning behind it, because the only other person to ever warn us about it was Junior."

"Trojan Horse, my ass," I grumbled. "Who do you think told me about it?"

"So, you killed him?" Ash snorted. "You know it's taken me an insane amount of self-control and at least half a bottle of sedatives not to set you on fire, right?"

"So violent," I grumbled and pressed the ice pack to my face. "Tank's sending you intel, you'll get exactly what I get. You're not to look into shit, that's my job, oh, and I bought a yacht."

"How is that related?" King asked.

"Oh, trust me, it is."

"You hate boats." Ash pointed out. "Didn't you just learn to swim?"

"Son of a bitch, if one more Abandonato talks about my lack of swimming skills or boating skills, I'm going to build a shank out of a shark bone."

Ash burst out laughing. "Aw, bro, you gonna make shark bone necklaces for us?"

"That's thoughtful, both a weapon and a sign of friendship." King pressed a hand to his chest. "I'm super touched, man."

"Go to hell." I groaned. "Okay…" I tossed the ice pack onto the couch. "…just make it look like you roughed me up enough to kill me, oh wait, you already want to do that. Also, the yacht makes sense, and I bought a car for Bella."

"To run her over with?" Ash asked, cocky shit. "Because I think we draw the line with two murders in the Family."

I didn't even blink. "Eat shit, you dirty kettle."

"Isn't it the pot?" King asked. "I could have sworn it was the pot calling the kettle black."

"They're both dirty." I pointed out. "And you don't know

what I know and that's kind of the point, so just do what you will, within reason, so I can go back to Bella-brunch."

Both King and Ash whipped their heads in my direction.

A small, hateful smirk appeared on Ash's face. "That's not a word."

"It's German." I lied.

"No way." King shook his head. "You hate brunch, you hate eggs, you'll drink the mimosas, but you want to go back to Bella."

"I hate Bella." I lied. "You guys know as much as anyone that I would run her over with the very car I purchased for her, so stop giving me so much shit and—"

A throat cleared.

It was loud.

It was feminine.

My heart nearly stopped beating in my chest as Bella walked slowly into the living room of the mother-in-law suite. Her face had lost all color, all joy, everything that made her want to fight me or engage.

I saw it, in real time, the second I stole the very last shred of dignity she had in her body, of pride, of fucking hope, and I watched it hit the ground with a resounding crash that I would remember the rest of my life.

Ash and King immediately started punching me.

They were going to anyway.

I pretended to fight back.

But I lived for the hurt, better I suffer physically the way I just broke her emotionally.

Blood ran down my chin the way tears ran down her cheeks.

My blood was spilled so others wouldn't be.

Her tears were spilled, mourning what would never be.

After a few sucker punches to the stomach, a knee to the forehead, and another punch to my left cheekbone that had my jaw cracking, I fell to the ground.

Ash sighed. "Bella, we're kind of busy, did you need something?"

She didn't answer, she just walked out of the living room.

And kept walking.

"Shit," I grumbled from the ground, grabbing the ice pack again.

King joined me. "You breaking her by accident is worse than when you did it on purpose."

I squeezed my eyes shut. "I don't know how to be the Trojan Horse in this scenario without breaking everything."

Ash tossed me a clean towel. "Nobody ever said you had to be the Trojan Horse to your partner in crime, and if what you're saying is true and isn't another ploy from you and the De Lange Family, we have a mole on our hands."

I snorted out a laugh. "Oh Ash, that's hilarious, you don't have a mole, you have someone out for blood, could be anyone, but one thing is certain, they'll take me out first so try your best not to be first in line to kill me, you kind of need the Trojan Horse," I pointed at myself. "In order to find the weakness, and right now, all eyes are on me."

"He's right," King added. "This doesn't mean I forgive you for killing my best friend in cold blood, but this also raises some questions, why would he ask you for that?"

"I'm out." I stand up. "I told you what I was allowed to say."

"Whoa, whoa." Ash grabbed my arm. "By who? God?"

I jerked free. "By Junior, you dumbass, now send some

extra men to protect my ass, stop making fun of my new boat, and give me one of your best for Bella. They'll come after both of us before they go after everyone else."

"What? Like there's a line now?"

"Guess whose name is first," I whispered, "and you win a prize."

I pointed at the white horse tattoo on my wrist. "After all, when a family line is cleansed, they don't stop at the leaders, do they?"

The room fell silent.

King stood. "Fine. You got your men, now give us more answers."

I yawned. "Yeah, yeah, I have to spend more money before that happens."

"Because why?" King laughed. "You have everything you could possibly want."

"Because…" I tossed him the bloody towel. "It's the only way to hurt whoever's trying to hurt us within the De Langes. The Five Families only gave a stipend, and it's going to go to hell if I spend it all." I grinned. "Which I intend to do."

"…can't swim, but has brains, truly fascinating," Ash said under his breath. "Should we get him water wings for Christmas?"

"On that note." I flipped them both off. "Keep me alive, mm kay, you need your horse."

"Sadly," Ash said under his breath.

"Heard that," I said.

"SADLY!" King repeated. "For the people in the back."

I smiled despite feeling sore and like shit and went in search of Bella. By the time I stumbled back to the brunch table, it was empty except for Trace, her mom.

"Hey, where's Bella?" I asked.

She frowned. "She said she was going to go looking for you?"

"She found me," I said slowly. "But started walking back here."

Nixon chose that horrible moment to come outside. "Hey where's Bella? She left her phone and purse, and nobody can find her."

Shit.

I broke her.

She cried.

She thinks her life is over.

I thought about it.

About us.

And I ran.

CHAPTER
Twenty-Eight

ENEMIES DON'T JUMP OUT FROM BEHIND THE DARKNESS.
THEY OFTEN BOLDLY WALK AT YOU IN THE LIGHT.
—KING CAMPISI

Bella

I fell for it.

Like an idiot, I fell for it.

I went on a very pissed off walk, off property, yelling at security that if they followed me, I'd slit their throats and did the stupid human thing. I left my purse, I left my phone, I left my security, and I left every shred of pride I had and went to the cliff, the one that Ivan used to run to whenever we had family dinners, and he got upset.

"It would be so fucking easy." Ivan stared down the ravine. "How high do you think it is?"

It scared me when he talked like that; I mean, I hated him, and I threatened him, but I didn't want to truly end him. "I don't know, maybe a hundred feet until you fall into the tiny stream and hit rock."

He snorted. "Yeah, that's only a few feet of water, splat you would go, but you'd feel like, flying, for a minute you know? You'd feel free."

"Are you in prison?" I joked. "I mean, you realize you just walked away from a bougie brunch where they serve alcohol to minors and give you gold plates because they're pretty and blood can't stain them."

He barked out a laugh. "Never thought I'd look at gold and be like, oh cool, way easier to clean."

"It really is."

"Real gold doesn't tarnish."

"Kind of ironic, the bloodstains won't stay, but every time I look at those plates, I wonder how much people will remember of me when I'm gone, you know? Will I be just like that blood on the gold plate that gets wiped clean, or will I last, will I be the one drop that stays?"

I sat down next to him. "Do you want to tarnish then?"

"I wouldn't call it tarnishing. I would call it being remembered. Existing."

I sighed, tempted to lay my head on his shoulder. "I can't decide if that's tragic or foolish."

"Both." He jumped to his feet and looked down. "If I'm ever missing, just look in the ravine."

I scrambled to my feet and nearly fell back onto the dusty rocks. "Don't joke like that."

He shrugged. "Maybe it's better to own your own destiny than turn around just in time for the knife to get shoved into *your back, ever thought of it that way?"*

I smacked him on the arm, then pinched it for good measure, he could be such an asshole! "No, and you shouldn't either."

Why was I so angry at him for talking like this? I shouldn't care, but his truth scared me more than the reality of what we were living in.

He leveled me with an intense stare that I couldn't pull away from. "You've really never thought how much easier it would be to fly?"

I didn't admit it to him. How suffocating it could be, how suffocating it was, and how every day I just wanted to be free for one second, feel the wind against my face, control the end, not just pretend everything was okay when I knew it could literally change at any second.

"Promise me if you ever get to that point, you'll wait for me here first," *I said instead of answering.*

"Same." *He held out his hand; it was beautiful in the morning light.* "Promise me if it ever hurts too much and all you want to do is fly—you wait for me too, all right?"

It was one of the only times in our lives, we shook hands without fighting in the next few minutes. His hand had been comforting, warm, not too soft, and when we finally broke free, he stared down at it like something precious had just happened.

I shook the memory away, I'd always liked it here on the cliffs, it was a great spot to think but also it was away from the noise and all the chaos. It overlooked a ravine off of my dad's property and felt private, despite the fact that I knew nothing was private in my life, I wouldn't put it past him to have straight up satellite footage of the wildlife area.

In fact, I'd be more shocked if he didn't.

I took a deep breath and refused to think about the old Ivan; it was like every single time I saw a shred of decency in him or even part of the person I used to know, he would do something horrible or stupid or cruel.

Until an hour ago, I was stupidly holding out hope.

Until an hour ago I had the errant thought… what if? What if we could be more? What if I could make this work? What if by asking me to trust him he meant for me to wait for him too? For all of this to die down?

And then hope blossomed more with the way he interacted with my family, with what my mom said, only to come crashing down in a fiery storm when I walked in on him and heard those words.

I mean, I was used to it, used to his hate, but it was embarrassing and hurtful, it wasn't just the way he said it; it was that it was in front of Ash and King.

I felt weak. Stupid. Vulnerable. Unnecessary.

And for a weak moment I thought—what if I just flew?

What if I just flew away?

Would it really matter in the grand scheme of things? He only needed me for my name, for an alliance, the other Families were too focused on keeping the peace, and I was just… a pawn.

Not something I planned on becoming when I was a little girl. I wanted to be powerful; I wanted to be like my sister, and now I just felt invisible, pulled into a war I never wanted to be a part of, and handed over to someone who would rather run me over, apparently with my own car, than hold me close.

I hugged my knees to my chest and stared out over the cliffs.

Dad would cry.

Mom would be devastated.

But this was the mafia.

What was one more death? I wasn't a boss. I wasn't anything.

The more I thought about it, the darker I felt, like my soul was finally coming to the same conclusion my head was, and both finally added up to the truth.

The world didn't need me in it.

The wind picked up around me, I stood, my heels crunching against the rocks and dirt, and I looked over.

"Long fall from here," a rough voice said.

I froze. I didn't recognize that voice.

It was gravelly, like the person speaking had something wrong with them. I didn't turn around, turning around meant I'd probably get pushed, well either way, I was probably getting pushed if this person meant any sort of harm.

"Yeah." I stepped to the right, closer to the tree that was planted on the edge of the cliff. "It is, but it's pretty."

"Lots of pretty things are dangerous," the voice said.

Finally, I looked over my shoulder.

They were wearing all black and had sunglasses on, a thick black scarf wrapped around their neck and a black brimmed hat that cast a shadow over their features.

They were around average height, a bit taller than me, and wearing black gloves. Never a good sign. Though the person had no weapon, then again, another bad sign, it meant they didn't want any evidence.

Thus, the need for an accident.

"Yeah." I stepped closer to the tree. "That's true. Are you out for a walk?"

"I'm out for a walk the way you're out for a walk." The voice laughed. "Do you want me to do it for you? It might be easier if it's your choice."

"My choice?"

"To jump." The person shrugged. "And let me preface this with, it's just business, it's only fair. Getting the Abandonatos out of the way and blaming Ivan just seems like the simplest way to start a little fight, don't you think? After all, you hate each other, of course he drove you to your death all in a selfish claim to the De Lange throne he claims he never wanted, now look at him, spending money left and right, acting like an idiot, and thinking he has a chance to stay when he's not even pulling the strings."

They were proud, this person, and they liked to hear themselves talk despite how painful it sounded.

I snorted. "You think I care about him? Or power? Besides, it's kind of amusing that someone else is pulling the strings… you? I assume?"

The person paused and tilted their head. "You would make a good boss."

"I'm my own boss." I forced a small smile. "And thank you."

"It's a shame."

"What is?"

"Your tragic ending."

"Yeah well…" I shrugged. "We can't all win, not even you."

The laugh that erupted from the face attached was sinister. "I always win, trust me, I deserve as much, besides my hand was forced. You know, the De Langes should have never taken the treaty. Junior lost his life because he got too close, what do you think will happen to Ivan? But nobody ever listens. He thinks he controls the Family. He wears the ring for now, but very soon I'll be cutting it from his finger, peeling it off and shoving the rest of that finger down his throat, let's pray it's a slow choking death."

I swallowed and looked to my left, nothing but a cliff.

The person raised their hand and crooked a finger.

A large burly man came down the path and stood behind them. "Push her, leave the note for her father, no messes."

"Yes, Boss."

Boss, as in another boss, not Ivan.

I didn't recognize the man; he had a scar running down his left cheek and he was at least six foot two, his dark hair was shaved close to his head, and he had a DL tattoo on his right cheek.

He was marked.

Marked like his own Family but apart from them.

I made a mental note and tried not to panic when the other figure started walking off. "Have a nice fall, you'll have at least four seconds to think about all your regrets, rest in peace, Bella Abandonato."

I swallowed and tried to think of a way to get out of my heels, so it didn't make it easier for him to attack me.

I backed up against the tree while he took a few steps forward, his blue eyes were dead, his mouth pressed down into a firm line. He wasn't wearing gloves; his hands were massive. There wasn't any time, he was already stalking toward me, maybe five steps away.

I tried to run to the left, but my foot caught on the root of the tree, I kicked off my heels and scrambled to my feet to run in the other direction when he was already on top of me, pulling me up from the ground.

I wrapped my ankles around his body and hung on for dear life. He'd have to fall with me.

He shoved a hand between us, but I pressed my head against his chest to keep him from creating space to pry me away.

"Get off!" He cursed.

My ankles were already slipping against each other, my feet went completely numb as I held on.

My first thought was that Ivan would be so pissed if I didn't fight and that dad would say he taught me better. Ironic that I had spent minutes wondering if they'd miss me, and now I wanted to live more than anything, even if it was to make Ivan's life more miserable.

I rearranged my arms around his neck, but it was enough time for him to gain space and slam down on my arms, sending me to the ground. I shoved my body back against the tree and stared up at him. Maybe I could crawl through his legs. I started kicking at him, when he suddenly went still over me.

Blood gurgled out of his mouth.

With a surprised grunt and a frown, he fell forward onto the dirt, right by my feet.

And Ivan stood behind him, knife in hand, blood splatter on his face. "Are you okay? Are you hurt?"

I opened my mouth, but nothing came out.

Ivan got down in the dirt and pulled me against him. "Hey, it's okay. You're in shock, it's okay, just take some deep breaths, can you do that? In for four seconds, all right?"

I nodded against his chest, but couldn't suck any air in. Panicking, I started to hyperventilate.

Ivan pinched me on the arm, then pressed his hand against my chest. "Breathe, now."

Too pissed that he pinched me, I was distracted enough to breathe once, then twice while he rocked me in his lap.

I heard my dad's voice, then others behind him, but I didn't want to leave Ivan's arms. He started to stand, but I gripped his arms.

He immediately stayed on the ground with me and spoke without looking over his shoulder. "It wasn't one of mine."

"How do you know?" Dad asked, before trying to shove Ivan out of the way. "Are you hurt? Bella? Talk to me. Are you okay?"

I shook my head and clung to Ivan.

"Bella..." Dad tried again. "Look at me, sweetheart."

My exhale was heavy, shaky. "I'm—"

"She's in fucking shock, Nixon, give her some breathing space, she nearly got thrown off a mother fucking cliff, all right? Would you be breathing normal? I know she's your daughter, but she's my wife, so step back and let me take care of her while you figure out who the hell would dare do this, all right? We all have our jobs, let me do mine."

Nobody talked to my dad like that.

But Dad sighed. "I know, I know."

"Then go be useful away from here." Ivan snapped. "Seriously, she's still shaking."

"She's my—"

"Again, I know who she is, but you gave her to me, she chose me, so let me choose her back right now and hold her, stop wasting words because I'm not leaving this spot until she feels safe, okay? If I need to grab a tent and send for water, I'll let you know."

I smiled against Ivan's chest and clung to him tighter.

Dad got up and walked off as more men ran up and started talking with him.

"I feel that smile, you know," Ivan whispered into my hair. "Think he'll punch me later?"

"One can only hope." I teased.

His laugh was soft. "I told you to tell me if you were tempted to fly, I almost didn't catch you."

"I'm sorry."

"Next time, I won't be late."

I pulled away from him slightly, my eyes searched his, they were so green, so focused on me I almost got lost. "You could have just let him push me—"

His soft kiss silenced me.

He was kissing me.

Touching me in front of my dad.

Cursing was heard behind him, I half expected him to get pulled away from me, instead he kept peppering painfully soft kisses across my lips only to move to my wet cheeks.

I didn't even realize I was crying when we touched foreheads and he whispered, "I asked you to trust me. I can't do this without you—I don't want to. Don't make me fly too, Bella."

What was happening? I kept getting two sides of him; I liked both, but I needed this one the most. I needed it like air in my lungs.

"Swear." I held out my pinky finger.

"Swear." He gripped it. "Stay in front of me."

I frowned. "To block attacks?"

He smiled. "So, I don't get led astray. Every man needs a good partner to lead them, I do better when that person is you. I have around three seconds before I have to start being an asshole again, but I did pinky promise, so trust me? Please?"

I nodded.

He helped me up and turned around.

And as expected.

My dad punched him in the face.

And when Ivan crumbled to the ground, his bloody smile grinned up at me while he mouthed. "Worth it."

CHAPTER
Twenty-Nine

Pain reminds you that you're alive.
—King Campisi

Ivan

It was worth it, it really was getting punched.

We were quiet on our drive back to campus; I reached for her hand, but only in the car.

She held on to it as we walked to our new suite on campus; we had the one bed because you know, married, and campus royalty and I still had to finish school and make things look normal.

Nothing to see here, just a mob boss getting his education by day and killing people during brunch.

It had to look normal.

Perfect.

Balanced.

Not just because of the nice people out to get us, but because any sliver of weakness and others might think they could pounce too.

Once we were in the suite, with its kitchen, living room, and huge king bedroom. I went to the bathroom and turned on the shower.

Bella was still covered in dirt.

She didn't even ask if she could come into the shower—she just stripped, dumping the clothes into the trash, not the hamper; then again, I realized she probably didn't want to be reminded—and stepped into the steaming shower, putting her head under it until she couldn't see.

I joined her. "Rules."

"You hate rules, you tried to burn almost every rule sheet given to us by the parents for like years."

I tried not to stare at her soft skin and failed.

"You're beautiful." I frowned when I noticed a faint bruise on her neck and pressed my palm against it. "Does it hurt?"

"No."

"Next time choke him out first, wrap second." I admonished. "Then again, he was really big, I'm proud of you for keeping a clear head."

She rubbed her eyes, mascara slid down her cheeks, she'd never looked so pretty. "Are you complimenting me?"

"It slipped" I licked my lips and backed her into the water again with my body, I lifted a shaky hand and ran it down her shoulder.

"Did that slip too?" She looked over at my hand.

"I'm very clumsy." I admitted, then lifted my other hand and cupped her chin. "We need rules."

"For?"

"Survival."

She took a deep breath. "How bad is it, Ivan?"

My chest clenched. "Nobody has really asked me that, not yet, despite the obvious information that I clearly never wanted this position."

"You lied to me."

"I lied to everyone," I said, meeting her gaze. "We have our own rules now. Mine is, I'll trust you, and I need you to trust me. I won't tell you everything because it keeps you safe, do you understand?"

She pressed a palm to my chest. "I would like to request an addendum to the first part of that."

"What?"

"Lie to everyone *but* me. Lie to the world. Lie to my family. Lie to your friends. But don't lie to me. You promised, you said to trust you, can I?"

"Yes," I said quickly. "You can."

"Do you hate me?"

I opened my mouth and closed it, then shook my head.

"Do you want to?"

"Most days yes." I laughed. "You said you wanted honesty."

"Why?" Her eyebrows scrunched up. "Why do you want to hate someone most days? I mean, I do want to hate you most days, but we all have our reasons."

When I looked at her, I saw someone I wanted to both love and hate, but they went hand in hand, to love her was to hate her, to hate her was to love her. The fear of admitting the vulnerability she pulled out in me was so heavy, so strong. I hated what her Family did, so I wanted to hate her too, because any other emotion meant—well, that I was sleeping with the devil, that I'd somehow failed.

And after that night, with Junior, after the killing.

She'd been the only one to see me.

I pulled her into my arms, her breasts slid against my chest, she felt so right in my embrace as I spoke against her ear. "That night, when I came back to the room and was bleeding, the first time, and you made me take a bath and I pulled you in, and I—" I stopped myself. "I let myself go with you, I let myself rely on someone else and you were so willing to be that person that I hated myself for being weak, and then I hated you for letting me."

"Weakness isn't in relying on others, it's in trying to do it yourself," she said right back. "You were my first kiss, you know."

"I know."

"You're a total asshole."

"That's been established, yes."

"Why did you kill him?" she asked next.

"Nice try with the quick questions, but that is one that I won't answer honestly. Now that we've made an addendum, don't make me lie," I said. "That's all I can give you."

She wrapped her arms around my neck. "Fine. Then I'm okay with your new rules. Now, I need you to tell me everything. You could have saved us a lot of pain and just let me in. I can act."

"You can't, actually, act to save your life." I pointed out. "You literally got kicked out of the Jr High play and had to switch parts with the apple tree."

"I got my vengeance."

"You ruined the play by throwing apples at the person who

stole your part." I laughed. "Then again, it was hilarious, you went up in respect that day in my fourteen-year-old mind."

More water dripped down her cheeks. "Why thank you."

"But no, keeping you in the dark keeps you safe, just keep doing what you're doing, acting like you want to kiss me and punch me at the same time, it's distracting, plus…"

"Plus?"

Shit. I was losing my own battle, wasn't I? "Plus…" I ran my thumbs over her eyes, they came back with mascara and water. I loved it. It felt real having her in the shower with me, it wasn't about having sex with her, or trying to control anything.

We were simply.

Talking.

No, no, we were flying.

I finally had my partner, my wingman.

"You're distracting. To me. Too." I could have easily made that sentence sound better as her eyes moved from mine to my mouth. See? Distracting.

She slid her hands up my back, then down again. "I'll forgive you for being a hateful jackass as long as you warn me before you mock me in front of others. I know you're trying to play the ass, but you keep hitting every single thing that makes me insecure, and it's going to be hard for me to remember that—"

I captured her lips with my teeth, then softly bit down and kissed her. Her tongue was so soft, so tentative, as it slid into my mouth.

I was showing her who I was without words, because my words had been hurtful, mean, I could at the very least show her in my actions.

She pulled away enough to look up at me. "What about the no touching or my dad kills you rule?"

I kissed her again. "I'm already dying."

"Aren't we all?" she joked.

I burst out laughing and pressed her against the tile wall when the sound of the door to the bathroom opening reached my ears and a throat cleared. "I swear if that's Tank, I'm going to slit his throat."

"Ivan?" Tank's voice sounded. "King has some news about the face tattoo, he'll be here in a few minutes, thought you might need some time to… you know dry."

"Mother fuc—"

"Shhhh." Bella clapped a hand over my mouth. "Remember the rules, I'll just finish up in here while you go get…" She gulped and jerked away from me and looked down. "Presentable."

"Presentable, my ass," I growled, then kissed her again, only to turn around, then back and kiss her again, and throw the shampoo against the wall. It made an echoing thud before falling to the ground.

"Ivan." Tank looked away when I walked out. I glared at him and kept walking, then slipped and nearly fell against the wall. "It's slippery."

"I know!" I yelled, only to slip again and nearly break my thumb. "Whatever."

I smiled when I heard Bella's laughter.

Before, I would have been annoyed that she was mocking me.

But that night, I smiled, because she was free.

CHAPTER Thirty

We're all blind to ourselves, to others.
The only solution is admitting it.
—King Campisi

King

"I'm a bad father. I'm my father. I can't win in this scenario." Nixon paced in the dorm waiting for Ivan, only to turn on me and shove his finger into the air like he was getting ready to use it as a weapon. "He touched her!"

"You're yelling."

"I'm FULLY AWARE of what I'm doing." His black suit looked rumpled, which was never the case with Nixon, he was always put together. He'd pulled off his jacket, tugged at his tie, and now he was in nothing but a white shirt, sleeves shoved up to his elbows, his pants, and shoes that kept slamming against the wood floor like they hoped to turn it into kindling.

I jerked my head toward the black leather chair in the corner. "Maybe take a seat while we wait for him?"

He kicked at the same chair twice, then sat. "I don't want to sit!"

"And the alternative is hitting someone or something?" I asked. "I mean, he saved her life, she would have died without—"

"I know."

"He killed Junior, who was like a son to you, I understand your anger, and she's your youngest daughter."

"Stop being the voice of reason, King. It really pisses me off more, it reminds me of myself being the voice of reason with others when they lose their shit." He fell back into his chair and pinched his nose. "I think he loves her."

My eyebrows rose. "I'm sorry, what?"

"He's playing me. He's wanted her from the beginning, he's playing a role, he knows things, Junior knew things. I'm not stupid, but it's my—" He took another deep breath. "She's my everything, my Family is everything, he's going to get her hurt."

"That," came Ivan's voice, "isn't your choice now, is it?"

Nixon jumped to his feet. "I said no touching!"

Ivan slapped his hands away. "Yeah okay, Dad, I'll be sure not to touch her after a near death experience with some monster and his cheek tattoo, good advice."

"Don't call me Dad."

"Don't make yourself look stupid." Ivan spat.

I whistled and looked away just as Ash came in and started to back out, only to have Phoenix shove him in the rest of the way. Maksim was chatting with everyone else in a separate room about our intel. I wanted everyone in here discussing the safest way to protect Bella and Ivan.

Nixon… was not helping.

"So…" Phoenix looked around the room. "This looks like a party."

Everyone turned to him.

He held up his hands. "Sorry?"

"She was scared, so I hugged her, I was petrified so I kissed her." Ivan spat. "Deal with it, Dad!"

"Stop calling me Dad!" Nixon roared.

"Dad, Dad, Dad, hey Dad, what's going on, Dad? What's your damage, Dad? You're doing too much, Dad, relax…" Ivan grinned. "Dad."

Nixon charged toward him, Phoenix blocked him and nearly got clocked in the face.

Maksim poked his head through the door, saw the drama, and backed away and closed it.

I sighed and glanced over at Ash. "You wanna start?"

Ash tossed a black folder onto the table. "I think Phoenix should."

The room fell silent.

Phoenix walked over to the folder and stared it down. "Do I want to open this?"

"Do you want to avenge your dead son?" I snapped just as Chase walked in, expression pale. "Open the damn folder."

Phoenix looked at it, then back up at Nixon and Chase. "I didn't want you to find out this way."

"Find out what?" Nixon asked. "That Ivan's a jackass and that we have a killer on the loose that thinks they're a boss and keeps branding their own men?"

Phoenix took a deep breath. "There were five."

"Five?" Nixon repeated. "Five what?"

"Over twenty years ago, there were five De Langes that Chase and I didn't cleanse. Five that disappeared off the map."

Ash leaned forward while Chase cursed and looked down at his feet. "And you think they're pulling the strings?"

"I think…" Phoenix sat "…that my son discovered them, and they made him pay for it, they wanted one thing, the money and the power, they wanted him to be a figurehead, I'm assuming. Knowing Junior, he said no, and they threatened his Family."

"Why wouldn't he just come to us?" I asked. "He knew better."

"You don't rat out a rat." Phoenix sighed. "You lead them slowly with their own obsession… he couldn't use force, they'd run, regroup, retaliate."

I nodded my head. "He wanted them all out exposed, in the open."

Phoenix tossed the black folder onto the table, the pictures slid out. Of Junior training Ivan, of Ivan's first kill, of Ivan becoming made and Junior's right-hand man.

"What better way," Phoenix whispered, "to pull out the rat from the darkness, then having your favorite betray you?"

One of the pictures was covered by the folder, I pulled it out and did a double take. "Wasn't his throat slit?"

"Junior?" Nixon asked. "Yeah, from left to right, couldn't miss it."

"He had a white horse tattoo on the left, not the right." Hands shaking, I dropped the picture while Phoenix stood and ran his hands through his hair. "Anything can be edited."

Nixon narrowed his eyes. "Ivan, are you still saying you killed him for the spot?"

"Yes," Ivan snapped. "Of course I did."

Nixon actually smiled. "He's vehement about it." I tilted my head. "Always is, about things you want, love, hate."

Ivan went still.

Nixon stood. "Good meeting. Keep your secrets, I'll keep mine, and Ivan, you touch her again without my permission and you'll pay for it."

Ivan reached for Nixon and gripped his arm. "With my life or with pain?"

"Why are you asking?"

"Answer the question."

Nixon cursed. "Pain."

"So I'll live?"

"You hate her."

"So I'll live," Ivan repeated. "Correct? On your word in front of our Capo. I'll live."

Nixon sneered. "You'll wish you're dead."

And for the second time in twenty-four hours, I witnessed Ivan whisper, "Worth it."

CHAPTER Thirty-One

Everyone has a secret. Everyone has pieces to that same secret. The hard part is getting everyone to finally show their cards. After all, we all have something we want to protect.
—King Campisi

Bella

It took him forever to get back.

Tank had been guarding the door.

And I'd been laying down in bed desperately trying to sleep without having nightmares of getting attacked.

The door to the bedroom opened. I had an early class in the morning, so I really should be sleeping and going on like everything was normal.

But he was back.

He was there.

In our room.

This sudden, massive presence, and he smelled good, though the air around him felt exhausting.

"Bad meeting?" I asked.

"Good news," he answered. "I might not die if I touch you, so can I please do one thing?"

I could have sworn my entire body lit on fire in that moment, though I played it off. "Oh, what?" I fake yawned.

"Can I hold you?"

I wanted to be held, but I wanted so much more, I finally wanted to just… do something for me, maybe for us. I was too confused to make any big decisions, so I didn't answer, I just turned on my side and let him pull me against him.

It was nice.

"Tell me about our first kiss," Ivan whispered against my neck, his lips sliding down to my collarbone, goosebumps erupted all over my body. I shuddered against him. "All I know is that I was in a bathtub, wet, and bleeding, and you were—perfect."

"Lie or truth?"

"Truth!" he said quickly. "Total honest to God truth, I hated you for it."

"For being perfect?"

"For being out of reach, for being the daughter of a Family that murdered mine, for being part of something I wanted to be a part of despite my guilt, for being pretty when you smiled, for helping me when I didn't deserve blood to be cleansed from my body—for looking and seeing an actual soul."

"A dark one."

"So dark."

"I was never afraid of it." I pulled his arms around me and pretended everything was going to be okay, that this was normal when it was anything but.

His lips tickled my ear. "Of what?"

"The dark."

"So, is that your way of saying you were never afraid of me?"

"Never afraid. Maybe more afraid of myself."

"Because you were afraid you'd get in trouble for stabbing me?"

I shrugged and looked over my shoulder. "Or maybe I'd get in trouble for actually kissing you instead."

"And if I would have begged you to save me from drowning in the darkness, what then?"

I turned to face him. "Maybe I would have told you I'd drown right with you, the only way to the other side is through the darkness—only then can you find the light, you know?"

"Found it." He kissed me, his hands tangled in my hair. "I found my light. I'm just terrified I'll be the same one to both find and extinguish it."

"Is it bad?" I asked again.

He pulled away. "It's not good."

"And Junior?"

"Next question."

"Are we going to die?"

"I hope not. But this person is… elusive, and they have a lot of power, control, it's like they've waited for years, we're drawing them out, but until then, we wait."

"So, suspect everyone."

"Basically."

"Live like there's no tomorrow."

"Absolutely."

"Love me."

"What?" Ivan jerked back. "What did you just say?"

"Love me then." I couldn't believe I was saying those words. "I mean, if we die tomorrow, you'd regret it anyway."

He sat up; the covers fell to his waist; the moonlight did all the favors to his gorgeous muscular body. He ran a hand through his thick hair. "No, I don't think that's the best—"

"I'm a virgin."

"Shit." He hung his head in his hands. "I'm going to go sleep on the couch, not because I don't want to be here in this general space." He made a grand motion with his hand across the bed. Adorable. "I just don't think this is the right path for us to take since all paths apparently lead toward death and one day you'll find someone that's going to love you the way you deserve. I can hold you, but I won't take things from you, I was honest about that promise and—"

I jerked up. "What?"

"What what?" He sighed. "I'm just saying I'm not going to—"

I slapped him across the face.

He lunged for me and slammed me down against the mattress. "The hell Bella!'

"You're leaving?"

A hot tear slid down my cheek, it burned as it fell off my chin onto my chest.

He squeezed his eyes shut. "Please don't ask me anymore."

"Do you expect to live?" I asked anyway. "Do you expect to live to see my next birthday?"

He was quiet.

"You promised." I reminded him.

He pulled away from me. "Get some sleep."

"Ivan!"

He stopped at the door and hung his head. "No, Bella. I don't have that high of expectations. And I refuse to wish for more than what I've been given, so maybe let me hold you next time, give me at least that."

The door shut quietly behind him.

I burst into tears over the man I hated.

I cried over the man… I was coming to love.

CHAPTER
Thirty-Two

You never go to bed thinking you'll wake up and it will be better because oftentimes, it's so much worse than you could possibly imagine.
—King Campisi

Ivan

Most nights ended up that way, with us talking but avoiding the questions we both knew I couldn't answer.

For the next week, at least, I had the great privilege of holding her and memorizing the sound of a voice I used to hate, only to come to the conclusion it would be the last thing I heard when I left this earth. A gift.

I held her.

She actually let me.

And things became almost unspoken, she never asked me a question she knew I wouldn't answer, and I only answered in truth and told her when I couldn't.

I'd like to say that my insane spending was pulling people out of the woodwork, that we knew more now that the whole tattoo thing came up, but the only lead we had on the tattoo was from years ago when the De Langes were working with the Russians.

Which only brought in more bosses, more Families, more drama, and more intense family dinners.

Exhibit A.

"Stop!" Andrei yelled at his daughter. "He's your husband!"

Santino blinked over at Andrei. "Cheers."

"I'm sorry. She can't help it. She clearly has my temper." Andrei agreed.

Phoenix sighed and poured more wine. "Like father like daughter."

"I think that was an insult?" I offered.

All eyes fell on me.

I needed an escape.

I didn't want to do this anymore, to hide in plain sight.

Knowing what I knew.

Sitting at family dinner.

Staring across at the familiar faces that saved my life, saved my bloodline despite trying to annihilate it so many times—knowing the truth.

The truth.

Seeing the documents.

Pouring over the videos for days.

Feeling the pressure of resurrection in a way that I'd

never fully realized until I went to reach for a roll, only to have Phoenix steal it from me and stare me down like he knew I knew his secrets.

He bit into his slowly.

I chomped mine down and shrugged like I didn't give a shit.

But I knew.

The heaviness of it was overwhelming. What the hell was I supposed to do? I wasn't a hero. They'd painted me a monster worth saving since I was cooperating and trying to find the rats in my own Family and now, I was supposed to somehow keep living a lie with a girl I actually cared for by my side.

She had no idea how much it helped, knowing she was there, but it also gave me nothing but shame.

I used her. Easily.

I provoked her on purpose.

And now I wanted what? A prize? A hug from her? The right to touch her? All because my feelings caught on fire and the world ran out of water to put it out?

She reached for her wine, her fingers shaking a bit when she grabbed it. Frowning, I put my hand on her thigh, causing her to apparently choke on her first sip.

I slid her white skirt up her thigh and traced. "U Ok?" with my fingers.

She grabbed my hand and wrote. "Tired."

I pulled her hand into my lap and started slowly rubbing my thumb over her fingers, then reached for my own wine and purposefully spilled it all over my food and my pants. "I am so clumsy."

I wasn't an actor, may as well just let them assume I wanted Nixon's daughter all to myself for a few hours.

I jumped up and grabbed Bella. "We'll go get some stuff to clean up."

King snorted into his orange juice while Ash shook his head and nodded toward Nixon, who had murder in his eyes.

At this point we had three tables, the younger ones were at those other tables, but the bosses always sat at the main one.

Yay me.

I shrugged. "I mean, if that's okay with you, Nixon. I would hate to upset you by taking my wife to get cleaned up after spilling wine all over the table."

"Wife." Ash repeated.

Not helpful.

It just reminded Nixon of all the things he didn't know, which made him want to murder.

"Actually..." King jumped to his feet. "...I have to chat with you really quick, why don't you send Bella to the bathroom while we go out back."

Shit.

The plan was to leave *with* her, not leave her alone to suffer in silence, a few weeks ago I would have spilled on her in order to get a rise out of her or you know get her to start swearing in front of her dad.

"It's fine." Serena spoke up for the first time at the dinner table. "I'll help her."

She practically fled from the table after putting Bam-Bam in Nixon's arms and kissing him on the head. Classic. He held out the toddler and sighed while Bam-Bam smacked him on the head.

Best kid ever.

I excused myself while everyone continued their talking

and followed King down the hall while keeping my eyes on Bella and Serena as they went to the bathroom.

"Wow," King said from ahead of me. "Weeks ago, you were watching her in order to find ways to tackle her to the floor." He frowned. "I guess you're still wanting to tackle her, but for entirely different reasons. Tell me, how is it being a eunuch? I've always been curious."

"Screw off." I shoved past him and opened the door to the back. We were at Phoenix's house, which just happened to have the perfect apple orchard surrounding it.

Rumor had it that the apples were poison, and that the orchard was built as a maze for hunting—the human sort, where you set the double-crossed person free and give them a few minutes to run or hide.

Hilarious, though I wouldn't want to be stuck out there.

King started walking toward the first part of the maze. Confused, I kept following him, I'd never been that deep in.

"Found some things out," he said, walking faster and faster. "But I figured you probably already knew that."

"What's this about?" I asked.

"Every man with a tattoo, according to our intel, has one thing in common."

I was afraid to ask. "Does it have to do with having the same last name?"

I was kidding. He didn't laugh.

"Your boy talked," King said. "Just like you said he would if we offered to sweep it under the rug and get him away from the Family for good, with his family."

I nodded. "Good. I assume that you told him I was the bad guy in this scenario and paid him off with Campisi money."

"Better." King ducked under a tree branch and kept walking. "I paid them off with Abandonato money, be sure to thank your father-in-law for that, in order to make you look even weaker, you're welcome."

"Ah, what did that set Dad back?"

"Meh, three mil, he'll barely notice it's missing, but I'd stay away from the house for a while because he knows you're the only one brave enough to access any of his funds."

"I mean, we are married, what's his is mine, right?" I joked.

"Yeah, please say that again, to his face, while he chases you around this orchard, I would pay to watch that."

"My death?"

"You'd survive for at least fifteen minutes, I've thought about this before."

"My death?"

"Nah, surviving Phoenix's crazy house."

I sighed as we walked into what looked like at least eight rows of thick poplar trees, the kind that were used in front of fields to block the wind and dust, were laid out.

King moved sideways through two of them. "Watch your head, and there might be spiders."

"Perfect."

"Kills in cold blood, still hates spiders."

I laughed. "Kills in cold blood, still scared of his wife."

King glared.

"What?" I grinned. "It's true."

"She's fierce, not scary." He pointed out. "And don't tell her I said that."

We walked through the eighth aisle until a small house came into view. It was maybe six hundred square feet and almost looked like an old logging cabin.

I crossed my arms. "So, you really are here to kill me and bury the body?"

"Nah, I just had a present for you, and I didn't want anyone to hear the screams, have fun, I'll send clean up later, but I figured this was the easiest way to prove your worth. You're the boss, now act like it and send them scrambling back to theirs with a message."

"What do they all have in common?" I asked while King started looking away. "Other than they're all De Langes."

King sighed and looked down at the grassy dirt. "They originally used to be personal bodyguards."

My stomach lurched. "To whom?"

"Mil De Lange."

And with that chipper news, he left.

CHAPTER
Thirty-Three

It's so much easier to be patient when you have a grudge. It makes the end so much sweeter.
—King Campisi

Bella

"Seriously, the stain's not that bad." I grabbed the black towel and started dabbing cold water on my white skirt. It was barely the size of a quarter; Ivan got the brunt of it.

I appreciated his attempt at saving me from sad looks around the table, it's like everyone knew I was with someone who didn't love me.

But I couldn't tell them the truth.

That at night he talked to me, that at night he held me and kissed my neck, that nights were becoming my favorite thing because they were normal, and I was understood.

I couldn't tell my family that he said to trust him, and he had to act a certain way just in case any of the men talked to the ones who were currently trying to take over the De Langes and eliminate us one by one.

Serena grabbed the other towel and started furiously wiping at a nonexistent stain on my shirt. "I need you to listen to me very carefully."

"Um, okay?"

"Sometimes, we're asked to blindly trust, and I think, no, I know that's what Ivan is asking you to do. But you have to decide, in the end, how far that goes. Will you trust him until you get caught in the crosshairs again or will you protect yourself? I need you to think seriously about this, when Junior—when he would come home from meetings it was constant fighting within the ranks of the men, a few spoke out, it got really ugly despite the many punishments that were given and then, there was money so much money that didn't add up and wasn't from any of the Five Families, when he found it he knew something sinister was going on and figured he was most likely the next target."

"And you're telling me this because?"

"Because…" Serena lowered her voice. "He never said goodnight."

"What?"

"That night, after date night, it's a ritual between us, he always tucks me into bed and takes care of Bam-Bam, he reads him a story, we've been doing that like clockwork since we had him and he promised that no matter what sort of meeting came up he'd always pop his head in and say goodnight and make sure Bam-Bam was okay. He didn't do that."

My sister was losing it. "Serena, he got killed, that's why he never said goodnight."

She shook her head. "No. No matter how many times I think about it, something isn't adding up, it's Junior, he's impossible to kill."

"Ivan was his protégé, Serena, he taught him too well and Ivan saw an in, you know how bitter he is." Why was I semi defending him?

He said to trust him.

I trusted in him and that something else was going on.

Serena leaned against the counter. "He's spending a lot of money, your husband."

"He's greedy."

"He's trying to piss off whoever's money that is, and he's trying to show them that he's not afraid, tell him to watch out, before he's next." Serena dropped the towel onto the counter and looked over her shoulder. "He might still betray you, even the strongest of bonds can be broken—for a price."

"He won't." I shook my head. "I know it."

"I hope you're right." She left the bathroom door open. My phone went off from the counter.

Ivan
I need you to meet me, take a left by the orchard sign, walk straight until you see the poplar trees I'm waiting on the other side.

Me
Okay.

I went down the hall and used the back door to the laundry room and started my trek toward the creepy orchard. During Halloween the first two rows were haunted, Phoenix made three kids cry—he didn't get the memo that clowns, however happy they appear—are terrifying.

He'd worked so hard on his costume too.

The fact that my dad dressed up like one too, was hilarious.

My stomach sank.

Dad.

Ugh, I felt torn between being loyal to Ivan and loyal to my Family, I felt caught in the middle constantly. I hated it.

I'd never been out this far, thankfully my phone would clearly still work if I got lost, when I saw the poplar trees, I said a prayer that all spiders would be dead and made my way through the rows.

When I got to the clearing, there were three men with blindfolds on and their hands bound.

Ivan was leaning against a tree, wiping his hands on a white towel. They were covered in blood, I'm assuming theirs by the look of blood running down all their chins and the gunshot wounds in each of their shoulders.

"Wife." Ivan grinned. "Do you trust me?"

His eyes were wild.

Something was wrong.

I didn't back away though the temptation was strong. He'd saved me before, this is a role he was playing, right?

"Husband." I cleared my throat. "Did you make me hike all the way out here to show me half dead men who most likely betrayed you or did you have a picnic planned ahead?"

"You can cut the shit, Bella, it's good for them to see what it's really like living with a monster. I figured the best thing I could do before sending them to Hell was give them a small piece of heaven and you know what thought came to mind?

I'll let you pick one to send back, the other two, I'll leave to you, so it's really in his best interest to go fast, besides I want to be entertained." He waved his gun at me. "Pick who gets to run the errand, the other two will stay with us until we get a text back from the person pulling the strings."

I swallowed, so he needed to prove a point then, I tried to stay logical. He needed one to go back and say he was crazy—that I was crazy too, or maybe even his victim. "And my role in this is to pick who to save?"

Ivan shoved away from the tree. "Do you think that your father or uncle made that choice? Do you think they took into account wives, children, needs? Or do you think they just slaughtered and killed an entire bloodline out of rage? Nearly making one of the oldest Families in the Cosa Nostra extinct?"

Tears welled in my eyes, they weren't for myself though; they were for the truth hidden in his own words. "There are rules."

"Exactly." Ivan walked up to me and wrapped an arm around my waist, pulling me close. His smooth cologne filled my nose while his heat surrounded me. "And one thing I did discover, one thing these men want the very most… can you take a guess?"

"Money?"

Ivan shook his head. "Abandonato blood," He kissed me across the cheek and laughed in my ear, his heated lips spoke against my skin. "So I offered them yours."

It made no sense, why save me only to kill me?

He was acting crazy though. I just needed to remember to trust him, to help him, at all costs. He'd asked me to hold him. He wasn't who he said he was. I clung to those memories, and the promises made in the dark. I clung to them like a lifeline, knowing if I was wrong, it would be my life on the line, and I would be dead.

Take the risk.

Walk down the aisle.

Make the choice.

You go through life thinking you have a choice, and you do, but what if the choice is you or them? What if the choice is to jump, knowing that you could potentially be jumping to your death, not flying toward life? There is always a choice, the question, however, will always be, will you risk it?

"Decide," Ivan yelled. "Decide who to send back Bella, and then I'll let the others get their cut of your blood, I would choose wisely, maybe the most injured should stay behind, they'll be easier to fight off, plus we do need proof I kept my end of the bargain." He threw his head back and laughed. "Wow, you should see your face right now, do you think for one second, I really give a shit about you? It's so easy to manipulate people, take for example, these pathetic men… so"—Ivan shoved one to the ground—"easy."

I quickly looked across the three men, noting their injuries as fast as I could, one was slumping forward more than the others especially after Ivan shoved him down. "He can stay." I pointed at the one and looked between the other two. One was smirking like he wasn't afraid to die, the other was serious, both looked strong, even sitting on their knees. "Him." I picked the one, not smiling. "He can stay too."

"So," Ivan walked over to the guy smirking and put his gun under his chin. "Looks like you're the lucky messenger. Be sure to let your boss know the meeting location and time, I'll be more than happy to hand over more Abandonato blood. I'll even agree to rip up the treaty and stop spending their money, but I want in on the cash, especially since they're going to be cutting us off once the treaty is void. I have needs too."

Wait, my Family was going to cut them off?

Huh?

"Is it true?" The guy's smirk fell. His blindfold was tight across his eyes. "Are the Abandonatos stopping the cash flow?"

I cleared my throat. I had to think fast, but all I saw was Ivan's sneer, so I closed my eyes and remembered his smile, his pain, his truth and spoke mine. "We don't support liars, and we sure as hell don't give money to traitors like Ivan. Dad said as long as he didn't touch me, he would keep supporting us."

Ivan grunted. "Please, it was just kissing, some heavy petting and—"

I smacked him across the face. "Shut up."

My hand stung, I gripped it and winced. "Aw princess, did that hurt? I can't wait to see you bleed."

"You're a monster." I spat.

"I'm a businessman." Ivan shrugged. "And I wanted my piece of you too, I can't help it that I don't have self-control." He kicked dirt up into the guy's face. "You have six hours to give your boss the message. You have my number."

He slowly tried to stand and nearly collapsed back on the dirt. "What about my men?"

"Oh, let them have their fun." Ivan jerked off the guy's blindfold. He was maybe in his fifties and had the same DL tattoo on his cheek. "It's not like she can't fight off two men, even someone well trained would struggle, if they die, it's on them."

He snickered. "Be sure to take pictures for our boss."

"I plan to." Ivan cut off the guy's rope. "Off you go."

He didn't need to be told twice. He slunk off in the opposite direction while Ivan took his knife to the other two men's ropes. "Play nice, I'll be inside."

He was leaving me.

Seriously?

He was really leaving me?

So I'd risked it all.

For a very low chance of survival.

He gave me his back.

But what did I expect? A hero when he clearly told me he was a villain? A man instead of a monster?

My dad would have killed the men before they even spoke innocent or guilty.

Uncle Chase would have made a game out of chasing them.

Phoenix would have cursed them.

The old Capo would have laughed while they screamed.

The list would go on about what my Family would do, Dante, Tank, Sergio, Santino, Dom, again the list went on and on and all it came to was one thing.

My cousins and I… we were different.

Programmed with the same strength as our parents, but more humanity, and I wondered if it's because they all sacrificed theirs—so we could keep ours.

What had I fought for?

I'd been perfect, and for what? To die? To feel sorry for myself.

An Abandonato they fought to the death, and I wasn't stupid.

I didn't deserve to be saved.

But I did deserve to save myself, whatever it took.

Ivan didn't look back as the two men faced me, they were at least six two, the one closest to me had both eyes nearly swollen shut, the other spit out a tooth.

I started slowly backing away. "Do I get a running start?" Where the hell was Ivan?

One of them lunged for me.

I ran to my right, putting the house behind me while they both took their time in walking closer.

I could maybe out-maneuver them, but I didn't have a weapon, I mean I had the dagger that my dad had given me that Ivan gave back to me, I always kept it on my thigh.

I reached for it and pulled it free, holding it out in front of me.

I really needed to do a better job remembering my training, remembering all the sparring with Ivan and how to take someone down twice my size.

"Relax, focus, you've already lost the cadence to your breathing," Ivan whispered. "It's embarrassing."

"You're embarrassing!" I yelled back, rubbing my arms.

Ivan laughed and then charged me, shoving me against the back part of the ring. "If someone tries to overpower you, you're just going to be exhausted trying to fight, give in a bit, use their momentum to turn the tables. If I'm charging you, let me until that very last moment. Watch."

He backed up while my breathing slowed.

And then he ran at me.

"One," I whispered to myself. "Two." His pace almost slowed as I moved to the left at the last second and slammed my hand

into his back, shoving him against the mat on the wall. "I win."

"And how do you finish this victory?"

"Huh?"

He spun out from the pin kicked under my legs and sent me to the ground, then pinned me there. "You always finish them, Bella, if your life is in danger you do not hesitate, you don't celebrate that you outwitted them for one second, you grab your knife and you go in for the kill, it's you or them, that is your choice and the only risk you're taking is fighting to live, or failing and dying. Do. Not. Fail." He got up from the mat. "I hate messes."

"How tender of you." I jumped to my feet.

He looked over his shoulder. "I may not like you, but even I know what you're worth, despite your insane inability not to see it."

I was so confused. "What?"

"Worth, not your family's money or your position, but your worth, what you contribute to the world, it's irreplaceable—you are irreplaceable, and that is how you walk into a fight, knowing your worth far outweighs theirs so why would you not possibly fight to the death in order to prove that."

I hated his words because I saw the truth in them and felt the weakness in my own convictions, so I charged him, I took him from behind and flipped him onto his back, wrapped my hands around his neck and I squeezed.

But Ivan just stared as if to say, do it.

When I jerked my hands free, he pulled them back down and placed them differently on his neck. "Next time I'll kill you if you do this wrong, hands further up, press your finger here, and your other here," His hands were still on mine when a tear slid from my cheek and kissed his.

We never talked about it again, about our cease fire, about him training rather than sparring, or about my tear, but we walked away knowing what it was.
Worth.
He saw mine when I couldn't see it myself.
And he taught me to fight for it.
It was either me.
Or them.
Nobody was coming to save me.
I could only save myself.

"Are you scared?" The one with the black eyes chuckled, his teeth were covered in blood. "Never thought I'd see the day an Abandonato ran off."

"Who says I'm running" I sidestepped him, then turned around and kicked him in the back of the knees while the other guy came barreling at me, he was more injured than the other guy so I used his body weight against him and waited until the last minute before sidestepping again and pushing him down to the ground knocking the other over.

Remember Ivan.

Use their anger, use their speed.

Remember Ivan.

Know your worth.

I shook my head. I needed to stay away from their hands and away from the ground.

I quickly grabbed one of the rocks by the door and slammed it down on the guy closest to me.

Cursing, he tried to roll out of the way; I grabbed another nearby rock. He immediately blocked his face while the other guy tried to crawl and get to his feet.

Once he covered his face, I dropped the rock, grabbed my knife and shoved it into the middle of his throat, and jerked back just in time to let the other guy stumble in front of me.

There was no escape.

He'd try to grab me, he was angry, not thinking.

I backed away like I was afraid until the house was pressed against my back. He lifted his hands to wrap them around my neck when I shoved the dagger into his gut and twisted.

He'd forgotten I had a knife.

And only focused on the fear in my eyes of being trapped.

With a gurgle, he fell forward, gripping his stomach. "You bitch."

The door to the house opened.

Ivan took in the scene and crossed his arms. "Finish him."

"You said we could spill Abandonato blood!" The guy rasped. "You lied."

Ivan grinned. "I said Abandonato blood would be spilled—not because you spilled it, but because she'll be the one spilling it herself—after she's made, you'll be her second kill."

I almost dropped the knife. "Ivan—"

"Bella, this is your birthright. You won fair and square. You want your revenge or do you want to let him go, he would have killed you, what will you do in this impossible situation? What choice will you make about your worth against his? Have you measured yet?"

Kill or be killed.

He was teaching me a lesson. Unbelievable! I could have died! It wasn't always an easy choice to make, kill or be killed. I thought back to Junior, to that night, and I knew, in my soul, it wasn't what it seemed. Kill or be killed, know your worth. He always knew Junior's worth, but not more than he knew his own.

Ivan's worth, in his opinion, wasn't high enough for boss, or to replace Junior, but if he was asked to prove that, I know without a doubt, he would even if it broke his heart, he would.

Seeing my hesitation, the guy lunged for Ivan, but I swiped my dagger across his throat before he could get closer.

He fell to the ground in a heap.

Shaking, I dropped my knife to the ground.

First blood. Second.

Made.

Ivan pulled a clean knife from his pocket, opened it and sliced it across his palm, then across mine, blood trickled down with the sting. Numb, I watched like it was an out-of-body experience as he pressed our palms together, our blood mixing while he whispered. "Welcome to the De Lange Family."

Holy shit.

I'd just gotten made by a De Lange.

By a De Lange.

My breath came out in a muffled gasp. I wasn't under Abandonato rules anymore, my only loyalty was to Ivan now, being his wife was one thing.

Being made by the boss.

Meant my dad couldn't kill him for touching me and couldn't say anything, it meant I was the one thing my dad would have never wanted me to be.

A foot soldier for the Family he tried to cleanse.

And partners with its boss.

He dropped my hand. "You did well."

"I killed two people." How was my own voice not shaking?

"You had no choice, and I wasn't going to do it for you," he said softly. "Besides, it was the only way to get them to agree, they thought you were weak, but I knew—you've always been strong."

He checked his watch. "Clean up should be here soon. Once I get the text from the dum-dum, we'll get going. Plus, he has a tail."

"Who?" I asked.

Ivan shrugged. "Believe me when I say I'm not that much of a mastermind, but I know others who are."

"Do you really think whoever this is, is going to actually meet you? Just like that?"

"Of course, because I promised to bring them all a little sacrifice."

"Who?"

Ivan smiled. "The entire Abandonato bloodline, excluding you, since now, you're legally—De Lange, should you thank me for saving your life?"

Chapter Thirty-Four

Trust is a fickle word with many meanings. You can trust a wolf because you see a sheep, and you can trust a sheep because you know the wolf.
—King Campisi

Ivan

I wasn't sure who was more traumatized, Bella or me, but it was the only way to protect her if things actually went horribly wrong with our meeting. It would keep her safe and it would keep her far, far away.

In the end, I guess being a De Lange wouldn't get a person killed, it would get a person saved, and keep a bloodline alive, even if I died in the process.

There was no chance in hell this person would step down, they'd take the crown from me once they got what they wanted and while I'd like to think I'm strong, the last thing I needed was to put my men in danger.

I could still survive today, tomorrow, but what about the next day, or the day after that? Eventually, they would come for me.

It was just a matter of when, unless my trick card worked out.

No matter how I looked at it, I would always be a target until eliminated.

Bella looked up at me, her green eyes held unspilled tears in them. "You did this to protect me, but not from my dad, even though it does both. You did this so that, so that if things go badly—"

"You're safe," I whispered. "That's all that matters."

I shook my head. "You're not."

"I don't think I've been safe since the minute I was born, Bella, and that's the truth. Just being a De Lange means bad things, let alone taking over the Family and pissing everyone off oh and betraying the other Families in order to draw out a rat, there's that too."

I grabbed her hand and pulled her inside the small cabin. It had a queen bed in the corner that doubled as a couch, a fireplace that was void of any firewood. A small kitchen with a brand-new stainless-steel sink, and a fully stocked fridge. "King wanted to make sure we had food."

"For what?" Bella followed me through the house.

Damn, she was so pretty. "For our honeymoon. It's only going to last a few hours, but when I was thinking about what I really wanted before my impending possible death, it was you."

"Me," she repeated. "And you aren't dying."

"The odds of me dying are extremely high, but I knew that coming into this. There's a bathroom and a change of clothes if you want, I'll get started on some food and wine, I figured we really could have that picnic."

"With dead bodies out front?" Bella pointed at the door. "Seriously?"

I checked my watch. "They're probably already gone."

"What?"

"See for yourself, I told King it wouldn't take long, and I was right, he offered some clean up."

"You guys are diabolical." Bella stomped toward the door and opened it, sure enough, both bodies were gone, and bleach had been poured all over the cement leading up to the house.

I peeked my head over her shoulder. "Yup, they're good at what they do."

"So, they know what's going on." She kept staring at the empty spaces. "And they're okay with you just possibly dying?"

"Sacrifices must always be made." I repeated what Junior had told me. "You asked why I wanted this, why I wanted to be boss, I lied that time." I turned around and walked back into the house. "I said it was for money, for power, for revenge…" I stared out the window facing the back of the property, more trees, and a small porch with a black swing seemed to stare right back. "Do you want to know why I took the role of boss?"

Bella was quiet, so I figured I'd answer her anyway.

She hadn't moved from the door, maybe she would run, I wouldn't chase her, my job was done already in keeping her safe.

"Why?" Her voice filled the room, even though she said it in a near whisper.

"Because, I wanted to change my fate, change the fate of the De Langes and when I was offered that chance, to actually do something worthwhile knowing it could kill me, I couldn't say no, especially when it was Junior who asked me to do it. He said we're all faced with impossible choices, it's what you do in those moments that define you, I chose my path knowing what the future risks could be, and I never regretted it once, because you told me you trusted me and I believed you."

"Because." Bella's voice was closer, her footsteps neared. "At the end of the day, no matter how many times I wanted to set you on fire—I did. I knew you would always save me when I couldn't save myself, and you knew I'd take a bullet for you while yelling at you for being stupid."

I hung my head and smiled. "It's always at the end of your life that you find your meaning, or is that too depressing?"

A smack landed against my back, then my head. I ducked and turned around. Bella had her hand lifted again.

The red wine stain was still on her white skirt, her matching white blouse had blood on it, her eyes were fierce, angry. "Keep talking and I'm going to keep hitting."

"I'm used to your violence."

Her eyebrow arched. "Oh?"

I rolled my eyes. "Christmas 2019, you waited outside my room for two hours in an elf costume, and didn't hand me a bag of coal, more like swatted me with it then put three more bags under the tree, naming each of my sins, whore, being one of them. It was lovely, thank you."

"You slept around."

"I never slept," I teased.

"SEE!" She raised her hands into the air. "Whore!'

"You're too easy. Do you really think I was sleeping around that much? Come on, I wasn't that bad, everyone goes through a stage in life."

She rolled her eyes. "Multiple times?"

"You're cute when you're jealous."

"I'm not."

"Are." I reached for her. "Come here."

She stepped away. "Nope."

"Come on, give a dying man a hug."

Tears welled in her eyes. "Don't say that."

"Sorry." And I meant it. "Let's just have the honeymoon we never got and enjoy each other until hell comes raining down on our Families and I make myself an even bigger target."

"Ciao." She crossed her arms and took a step toward me.

"What?"

"The first thing you said to me was Ciao, Bella, followed by numerous insults and stupid boy things, but I could never understand if you were saying hello or goodbye."

"Open ended," I admitted. "Because I wanted to say hi, but I was afraid that the minute I did, I'd be saying goodbye, so I figured it covered my bases. That if something happened to me, I wouldn't be sad because I said goodbye first."

A tear spilled onto her cheek. "My first goodbye, my first kiss, my first marriage, my first honeymoon, how many firsts are you willing to give me Ivan De Lange?"

Blood pounded in my ears. "How many do you have left?"

I knew the answer.

I wanted to hear her say it.

"I think I have one you might want." She wrapped her arms around herself. Was she being shy? She took another step toward me then pulled her shirt off, her nude bra barely covered her breasts. I gulped hard when she slid out of her skirt and kept walking toward me.

Was this really happening?

I should tell her to stop, I should explain that my self-control was next to nothing after holding her every night and that I never fell asleep fast but tortured myself with thoughts of kissing her, stripping her down, making her truly mine.

She stopped in front of me, her breasts grazing my chest. The cloth was so thin I could feel her heat through my shirt. "I mean, I've never taken a shower on my honeymoon in a cabin, I guess that's a first."

"Y-yes," I agreed. What the hell? "It is."

What went on beyond that for the next hour, I could only describe as hell. She took her shower, loudly, and asked me to find the soap after getting too much in her eyes and needing help to rinse off.

She was naked, I nearly ran into a wall.

"Another first!" she'd yelled after showering. "Romantic dinner by ourselves without any security."

"Yay." I started grabbing some of the meat and cheeses in the fridge and nearly choked when she walked out of the bathroom naked. "Let me guess, another first."

"I've never just walked naked in a cabin in front of my husband."

"Great."

"Oh look, a book. I've never read a book naked."

"Do it all the time." I lied. "There should be something over there. I think." She was slowly killing me.

"Also…" She grabbed some old book and opened it. "I've never done one more thing."

Please let it stop, I couldn't even focus on what was cheese and what was meat anymore on the wood board, it looked like a toddler got into the fridge and was trying to build a shrine.

She hummed happily to herself while I checked my phone and read back through the messages again.

> **Me**
> It's done.

I'd texted King first, then Bella.

> **King**
> What will you do?

> **Me**
> Stick to the plan, my guy's following the old bodyguard just in case the new boss double crosses us or doesn't want to meet, at least we'll have a location.

> **King**
> And Bella?

> **Me**
> I'll make sure she's protected—made—into the De Lange line and pray I don't get killed later.

> **King**
> The cabins stocked, use your time wisely. You won't have much of it, but I'll cover for you before we break the news to everyone that you've betrayed the Five Families and have her as a hostage.

> **Me**
> She'll come willingly.

> **King**
> Try not to get killed.

> **Me**
> I thought that was the plan all along... besides, if I don't end this, then Junior's choices will have been in vain.

> **King**
> There's always a way to pull out poison—he chose the right one, we can't begrudge him that.

> **Me**
> And yet I'm still pissed at him.

> **King**
> Text Bella, Serena just left the bathroom.

We had all grown up amid violence and anger. Rage was all too often the first response to every situation. Danger was the norm. Even now, danger stalked us, sought to end us. Was there not something poetic in striving to claim a small bit of paradise within the chaotic hell that was our everyday life?

Don't think... feel.

I was so lost in my thoughts and that text conversation I almost didn't hear Bella sneak up on me, completely naked. The knife slipped from my hand, clattering onto the counter. "Sorry, what was that one last thing?"

Please say chess, play chess, and put on a blanket and stay completely covered in a corner.

"Play naked with my husband in the kitchen."

I braced my hands against the counter. "Sounds dangerous, lots of po+inty things."

She shoved the knife across the counter and dipped herself under my arms so that they were pinned on either side of her. "Take off your shirt."

I almost snapped, *you take off your shirt*, then realized

duh, her shirt was already off I was just losing my mind.

I slowly peeled my shirt over my head and dropped it to the ground. "Happy?"

She shook her head no. "Now your pants."

"Should we put on music?"

"Are you offering me a show?"

"It might cost you." I leaned in and captured her mouth. "Sorry, I slipped, I'm a clumsy dancer."

"I see that."

I kissed her again. "I have a condition where everything has to be done in even numbers."

I kissed her again. "Shit, I slipped again, that's three, so that means I need to go for four and—"

She wrapped her arms around my neck, fusing her mouth to mine. A possessiveness I'd never felt in my life took complete control of my body, it wasn't that I was running out of time; it was that I had her, I fully had her, and I didn't have to feel guilty about my word to Nixon.

Because she was mine.

And I'd done what I promised.

"Ciao, Bella," I whispered in my mind.

Hello.

Goodbye.

Hello.

Goodbye.

I loved both words, because they meant I'd met her in both scenarios and had no regrets leaving.

I pulled away from her. "I'll get the rest of the food ready."

"No." Bella grabbed my hand.

When I tried to pull away, she held on even tighter. "What? You aren't hungry?"

She placed my hand on her naked hip. "Are you?"

For so many things. "Bella, why don't we sit down for a bit?"

I had no qualms kissing her, pleasuring her, I would do everything to her—but the one thing I wanted the most, because in the end it felt selfish and wrong. Like the people who sleep together, then leave the next morning without a note. I couldn't promise her everything was going to be okay, or that she wouldn't be planning a funeral, so I couldn't take something that was important to her.

She shook her head. "My choice, dumbass."

"But shouldn't—"

She kissed me into silence, then grabbed both of my hands and put them on her breasts like I didn't know what to do, so plump, soft, I angled my head and kissed her deeper, pressing her up against the counter while she slid a hand into my briefs and tugged them down.

I cursed against her mouth, pulling free long enough to kick them away and devour her until I tasted all of her.

She kissed me the way she liked to fight me, with every ounce of energy she had, fighting for dominance while I picked her up and walked us back toward the bed.

I set her down on the blankets, refusing to break away from her mouth as she lay back and took me with her. Our hands tangled and our tongues matched like we wanted to be wrapped up in one another.

Heart pounding, I reached between us, swallowing her moan with my lips, keeping each sound with me like a stolen gift.

Panting, she pulled back from me, sliding her hand

between us, batting mine away and gripping me, then guiding me to her entrance. "Ciao, Ivan."

"Is this hello or goodbye?" I was afraid to ask.

"Hello." A tear ran down her cheek. "Goodbye isn't in that definition of ciao, I looked it up."

"Did you now?"

"Yup, they updated it."

"And you noticed that in that book you were reading upside down earlier, hmmm?"

"It may look old, but it has a lot of secrets." She kissed me and held me so close that it was impossible not to move.

"Mmm…" I kissed down her jaw. "This is going to hurt at first."

"I'm not worried."

"Why?"

"Because"–she cupped my face with both hands—"I trust you—I trust you with me."

I shoved forward, she let out a pained gasp. I went completely still. "Are you okay?"

She kissed me instead of answering; I moved as slow as I could, with each thrust I felt her relaxing more and more until she pulsed around me. I could feel it like my own release. I leaned down and tugged her ear with my teeth and whispered, "Ciao, Bella."

CHAPTER
Thirty-Five

*Always be ready for the worst-case scenarios,
they happen more than you realize.
It's not always a happily ever after, oftentimes, it's a funeral.
—King Campisi*

Bella

I was full. Full of him.

I didn't want him to leave. He kept kissing me, kept moving, and when his body shook over mine, all I saw was his beauty and dedication to me. No matter what, he had been loyal to me. He'd taken care of me, regardless of what could or would happen to him.

He sacrificed for his Family.
For mine.
For me.

He wasn't the hero people expected; he was the villain everyone needed.

His head lowered, his dark hair covering part of his bright eyes in a way that made him look even more mysterious, while his biceps flexed on either side of my body as he held himself over me. "What?"

"You're pretty."

He snorted out a laugh. "Wow, sex and compliments? Sign me up."

"New rule," I said. "You know, after we get out of all of this without dying and saving the world."

"Naturally."

"…Always say hello and goodbye. No matter what."

"Every day?"

"Every day. I want my days to start with Ciao, Bella, and I want them to end with Ciao, Bella."

He kissed me on the nose. "As long as I'm alive, I promise."

"So, stay alive."

"Not really keen on dying, Bella, but what's one small sacrifice to save the many, you know? I mean, I wish I could be that guy who's all 'burn the world, I'll just save her.' But that's a romantic idea that, in the end, I can't stand beside. Too many people have already died, so if it happens to me, don't think I went out all sad, think of it like a celebration. Think of it, like winning."

"But I'd be losing."

"But everyone else would be winning." He pointed out, eyes sad. "Your dad, your mom, your sister, Bam-Bam, we can't let this person gain even more of a foothold in the Family, they're obviously powerful enough to try."

I took a deep breath. "Let's eat, then come back to bed."

"To cuddle?"

"Yes." I laughed. "I'm going to cuddle you so hard you get me pregnant."

He quickly looked away. "Nothing, it's nothing, just, the past never really stays there, does it?"

"Meaning?"

"It can't help but repeat. It really can't."

We didn't talk about it during our quick meal, or when we were tangled in bed again, kissing, and touching, laughing and living.

He distracted me so much I forgot to ask why that would make him think that the past was repeating itself. Why his words felt familiar.

And when his phone finally went off, while we were eating, I knew, I knew it was time.

I just wasn't sure if it was a hello or goodbye.

"We have a date." He jumped to his feet. "And the location, in case they don't show up. Time to send the text to your dad, look devastated."

It wasn't acting, not when he held up the phone and took a picture of my face, not when he sent the threatening text to my dad to bring the Abandonato line out or he'd slit my throat.

Nor the address where he said to meet them.

"What if he doesn't believe you?" I asked.

"King has the bodies," he answered without looking up at me. "He's telling them I'm going on a spree and you're next, a family line for a family line."

"And if he still doesn't believe you?" I asked.

Ivan set down his phone and walked over to the kitchen and picked up his gun from the counter and pointed it at me and fired.

"Ciao, Bella."

CHAPTER Thirty-Six

Sometimes a hello means goodbye.
—King Campisi

Ivan

I shot her in the shoulder, sending her crashing to the floor, then took a picture and sent it off to Nixon. I quickly grabbed a towel and tossed it to her. "Put pressure on it, try not to pass out."

"You could have warned me!"

"You could have flinched; I didn't want to hit an artery."

"Romantic."

"Yes, that was what was going through my mind while pointing a gun at the girl I've both loved and hated for forever, gee how can I make this more romantic."

She dropped the towel. "You love me?"

"Did you miss the hate part? I included that too."

"You can't have both."

"I demand both. I demand everything." I forced a smile and tried to stop shaking at seeing her hurt. "Now, put on some clothes and forgive me for shoving you into a nice waiting vehicle while we go have a family reunion."

"Ah, I get to put on wine stained and bloody clothes, yay me."

"It does add effect." I smiled at her, proud of her for being brave, for not yelling at me, but also for trusting me even to the end.

She quickly pulled on her clothes despite her injury and followed me outside the cabin. One of the black Escalades was waiting, engine running.

Tank hopped out and opened the back door. "For the record, I still feel like this is a shit idea."

"I concur," another voice said from inside. "Leave it to you to deviate from the actual timeline for the plan."

"I like ghost stories, shoot me… oh, wait." I laughed and got in, then turned around and winked at Bella. "One more surprise before my impending death."

Junior was sitting in the back with dark sunglasses on and a black Nike hat. "Hi, cousin."

The idiot actually waved.

Bella stumbled into the car and smacked him across the face, the sound was so loud I winced for him, only to have her do the same to me. "You assholes!"

"I missed you too." Junior sighed. "What's with her?"

"Told you she'd be pissed."

Bella burst into loud sobs and threw her arms around his neck, despite her injury. "What the hell is wrong with you?"

"I can answer that." I offered, earning a glare from Junior, who had tears in his eyes. "Or not."

Tank got back into the front seat. "I'm off to the location, Nixon has troops mobilized, King has everything set on our end, you're taking a gamble on this one, bringing him out like this."

"I was bait, now he's bait." I hoped. "Besides, they'll bring everyone, this isn't just revenge anymore, this is winning."

Junior held onto Bella. "I'm sorry. I'll explain later."

"Explain now." She smacked him with her good hand, her other arm was bleeding again, I grabbed the towel she brought with her and pressed it to her shoulder while Junior talked.

"So there were attempted murders on me a dozen or so times. Random people, not part of any of our Families or anyone I knew. I started digging, found out some unsavory things, saw the money, tracked it to some offshore accounts, couldn't figure things out without buying time, and I knew that they already had plans in place for more attempts on my life. I had no clue who to trust, who not to trust, and who was just waiting in the woodwork, but a new boss would throw everyone for a loop. There are rules, there's the treaty, there's trying to figure out someone's weak spots with erratic behavior, add in a funeral, and a wedding, and family visiting, and well, say hello to buying time, plus they did set me up to look like the number one betrayer of the Five Families so that was fun."

Bella frowned. "Then why is Ivan talking about his impending death?"

The car fell silent.

Tense.

"Bella…" I put my hand on her leg. "This Family needs Junior, it doesn't need me, I'm going in as a distraction, as bait, so we can take down whoever this person is."

She looked between us. "You guys are idiots! If your own men don't kill you, then my dad will! This is the worst plan you could possibly think of."

"Or the best." I snapped. "They have a joint enemy that needs to be eliminated, it again buys us time. Junior's going to join forces with Ash, King, and Maksim, while Santino puts men around the building. It's not foolproof," I explained. "But there's a vendetta here, trust me when I say whoever this person is, they want Abandonato blood, and they want it yesterday."

Bella sat back against the leather seat and put her hand over mine, pressing it against her wound. "Who would hate my Family that much?"

Junior whistled. "Any of the De Langes who got eliminated, I mean it could be anyone, even the Russians. Who knows? The point is, this was the one thing this person wanted more than anything. The Abandonato heads on shiny platters. Part of me even thinks they want it more than control of the De Lange line."

"The question is," I asked, "who would be that psychotic and stupid?"

I would find out the answer soon.

We pulled up to Chase's old house.

He'd moved out of it with Luc, it was kept on Abandonato property as an Airbnb, though right now it was empty.

"I used to love this place." Bella stared out the window. "But why here of all places?"

Junior looked down. "When I was pretending to be

dead, I did recon. It was one of the only places the men with the DL tattoos would randomly rent. They always came in with multiple cars and always had one person with them—guarded. Granted, it's a great location, incredible property, it could just be a coincidence. Either way, they'll feel like they're in their own native territory, not realizing we know all the secrets the property has to offer."

I knew the secrets.

I knew the horror.

I looked down at my hands. "We should have burned it to the ground."

"Chase wouldn't let us." Junior sighed.

"Why?"

"He said even ghosts need homes." Junior confessed, as a chill ran down my spine.

CHAPTER Thirty-Seven

To die, is to finally live.
—King Campisi

Bella

I followed Ivan out of the car, Junior stayed behind like promised.

I wasn't afraid of getting hurt, I was afraid of Ivan doing something stupid. "Don't you dare try to stand in front of me if someone shoots at me," I snapped.

He barked out a laugh. "Same goes for you."

"And don't fall on your own sword then give me this pathetic 'I should have had more time' sort of look, I want you to like, flip me off or something, go out angry if you go out."

He laughed harder. "Wow, so bossy today."

"Well, *she* just got shot, so excuse me for having no patience."

"She's strong."

"*She's* angry at you."

"For good reason. You're beautiful, by the way, just in case I never said it and acted like a jackass most the time, I always thought you were pretty, I was just afraid to show you a chink in my armor. Once an enemy, always an enemy."

I huffed. "You're okay to look at, I guess."

"I'm gorgeous and I know it. But thank you for attempting to humble me."

"This is what's wrong with you."

"Sweetheart, there is so much wrong with me, but can you be the one right thing? Aww see, that was nice of me. I'm getting good at this husband stuff."

A sharp pain hit me in the chest. He wasn't leaving, right? He wouldn't do anything stupid?

It was Ivan, though.

I took a soothing breath. "How far are we walking?"

"Just to the back, by the pool. I'm assuming they have people surrounding the place. I told your dad to meet us near the pool house, and oh shit—"

It wasn't just my dad. It was Phoenix, Tex, Andrei, Sergio, Dante, and Chase, along with what looked like about forty Abandonato men from my dad's side, and forty from my uncle's. All of them casually standing there like they were about to start a war.

"Hand her over." Dad pointed his gun at Ivan.

He cursed. "I said Abandonato, not the other Families, this has nothing to do with them." He cursed again. "Bella, you should have told me your dad was going to lose his mind and not listen."

"I didn't protect her from you once, I won't make that same mistake again." Nixon held up his hand, keeping his army at bay. His men had all of their guns trained on me, so many wonderful red little dots. "Bella, walk over to me, slowly."

"The deal," Ivan spoke in a calm, even tone, "was for you to bring all the Abandonatos, it's like you're just begging to cleanse all of the Families, is one daughter that important to you? One small person?"

"Yes," he and Chase said at the same time.

I didn't see the first shot; it was near Dad's head but took out one of his men. The second and third hit Chase's security.

Ivan shoved me to the ground. "Stay here."

I tried to grab for him, but a bullet whizzed by me. Around a hundred people in black camo were walking toward the group of us, with another person in similar clothing, wearing sunglasses and a hood covering their neck and head like it was freezing out.

They held up their hand. The bullets stopped. "Lovely family reunion, what a treat, I make a deal with the devil, and he more than follows through." They looked over at Ivan, who had gotten closer to the group. "You were useful, after all. I mean, you're going to die, but I think you already figured that when you lured everyone here for me using your little pawn of a wife." They looked over at me. "Should I kill her first?"

"Can't." Ivan held up his hands and stood dangerously close to my dad. "She was made last night—two of your own went to meet Satan, she's the one who sent them and as acting boss, I made her—into the De Lange line, so technically, she can't be cleansed."

"And what makes you think I follow rules?" The person glared, their voice was just as raspy as before, terrifying sounding, painful.

Ivan shrugged, hands still up. "If you really want control over the Family, you'll at least show that you'll honor De Langes. If not, you're just as bad as the guys standing in front of you. They did cleanse an entire Family line, well almost, since I'm still standing here. Point is, you'll need loyalty once you do this. You can't have your own men turning on you at such a pivotal point, can you? Oh also, when you pry the ring from my finger, you might need to size it down a few notches, you look—small."

The person pointed the gun at Ivan, then switched it to my dad and shot.

Ivan shoved dad out of the way and stumbled forward, it hit right below his neck on the right-hand side, barely missing his head.

And then the gun trained on me.

The sound of sirens filled the air.

What the hell was going on?

Ivan moved to his feet, leaning forward. "Shoot me again if you want, or I guess you can try and run, but the place is currently surrounded by the FBI." Ivan gave a mock salute. "Trojan Horse, bitch."

Hundreds of FBI agents swarmed the grass with Junior and Tank leading the way like it was a normal occurrence in our Family.

I mean, I knew we had ties with the FBI, and we helped one another from time to time and that different people had worked undercover for them, but what?

"Drop your guns." Tank held out his badge. "Now."

No way?

He was back in?

I thought he had to give up the FBI in order to marry into the Family.

"Good work." Junior patted him on the back.

Phoenix stumbled toward Junior.

But Junior shook his head and nodded to Ivan.

What did they know that I didn't?

Everyone dropped their guns but the person who had shot dad, they pointed it between Junior, Ivan, and finally landed on Chase.

With a sigh, Uncle Chase stepped forward and called off Junior, then turned over and nodded to Phoenix.

I got up and walked over to Ivan; he was bleeding, but not bad. "What's going on?"

"Well, it was kind of like the ending to Avengers, I just expected there to be more killing less talking, but I think, I can fully promise you to always tell you the truth now that it's about to be out. I'm sorry I lied."

"Huh?"

"Phoenix's rise from the ashes." Ivan wrapped an arm around me and winced. "And demons, never die."

The person wasn't putting their gun down, but it was shaking, genuinely shaking in their hands.

Uncle Chase stared the person down, unafraid of the gun pointed at his face and whispered. "Do it. I fucking dare you."

The gun pointed from Chase to Phoenix now.

Phoenix just shook his head, then finally looked over at Junior. "What do you prefer?"

Junior smiled. "I'm no longer the acting boss of the De Lange Family. Ask him."

All eyes fell on me, including that of Tank, who was still pointing a gun at this person's head.

"Be right back." Ivan kissed me on the head and walked away, I only hoped it wasn't to his death—again.

Chapter Thirty-Eight

*Revenge isn't just about getting even.
It's about making things right.
—King Campisi*

Ivan

I didn't believe it when I saw the text from King—directly from Junior. Proof. The proof we needed. The proof that stared me down in the face. I knew it would be volatile.

I didn't, however, know how bad it could have gotten with the rest of the men there watching.

Some knew the history of the Families.

Others whispered about it.

How the De Langes fell.

And today, I would be the one—to make them rise.

I stood in the middle. The gun moved to my forehead. I took a deep breath and realized in that moment, I had to make the choice as boss.

I wasn't trying to be the hero.

I was trying to be humane to someone who lost it all and never forgave themselves in the process, someone who carried the weight of the De Langes mistakes and, in order not to let it destroy them, embraced them in wait.

"Mil De Lange," I whispered. "Death would be too kind for what you did to our Families, for the mistakes you made and never owned up to, for the lives you willingly destroyed. You slid down the slope and forgot to ask for help to get out. That's on you, and I won't make the same mistake." I crooked my fingers to Tank. "Shoot me, shoot all of us, but it won't change what's about to happen, you're under arrest, may you rot in prison for using these Families against their own, and may the grace the Five Families are bestowing upon you right now, feel like the fires of Hell itself."

Her hand shook as she lowered her gun.

Chase impatiently swatted it out of her hand, and with shaking hands, pulled the hood from her face, her sunglasses went with it.

There was a jagged scar running down the left side of her face that ran through her throat in such a grotesque way it was hard to look at.

One eye was a milky white, as if blinded.

Her hair was pulled back into a tight black braid. She had aged from the pictures I had seen of her, but she was still striking in her own way.

"Why?" Chase tilted his head and leaned in. "You should have stayed dead."

"Says someone with a perfect life," she spat.

He shook his head. "One, I fucking fought the same way that I fought for everything and everyone I hold dear, the way I sadly and mistakenly fought for you."

She flinched. I wondered if stabbing her would have been kinder.

A tear slid down her cheek. "You don't know where they put me, what I went through, what I fought for to get back, to get to you." She reached her hand down to her thigh. "I love you. I loved you then, and now."

Her movements were slow, but she was quick when she pulled a knife from her hip.

She stabbed it directly into Chase's side.

He was wearing a bullet-proof vest—he always did now that he was a senator; I wondered if she would know even that about him. Probably not. Because in the end, she only cared for herself.

The knife clattered to the ground. He gripped her by the wrist. "I'm officially out of your reach, and I have been for some time. Enjoy prison and take one look around you at the empire we've built that you wanted to destroy down to your own Family. You want to know what love is? It's when you sacrifice everything for them, rather than sacrificing them, for yourself."

Tank stepped forward and put her in cuffs. "She escaped prison, with the help of a few of her men and was assumed dead after finding her clothes and some of her teeth near the burning escape car, one of our own was in on it and on payroll, they wrote up the case as death by burning and helped her re-establish herself."

Phoenix cursed, finally speaking up. "How long ago?"

"Two years ago." Tank revealed. "We just put two and two together this morning after Junior captured the picture and infiltrated. With King and Ivan's help, we were able to set this up. Well, that and Bella, who probably needs medical attention."

I stared down at Mil. "What? No last words before prison? No, thank you?"

"It was always mine," Mil rasped. "The De Lange Family was mine."

"Then you should have taken better fucking care of it," Phoenix snarled.

"I was going to fix it!" Mil screamed. "I was going to fix everything!"

I released a sharp laugh. "Didn't you know? We already did, without your help."

Chase was the first to turn his back on her, Phoenix second, and slowly every single person turned away, a sign of cutting that person from memory.

And finally, I did the same as Tank carried her away while she screamed.

"Did you know?" Nixon asked Phoenix.

Phoenix sighed. "I considered her dead as well. She just barely survived that day, but get one thing straight, she died that day, to all of us, and the dead should stay buried."

"Risky." Chase pointed out.

Phoenix shook his head. "I thought so many times to let you know she had made it and then when I visited her one last time, I didn't recognize her anymore. Her soul left that day. What you see now is a shell. It would have been more painful to give you hope that you could still save her when she was already gone, she spoke in riddles all the time, the injuries weren't kind and caused brain damage as well."

Chase nodded and pulled Phoenix in for a hug. "You did the right thing."

Andrei walked up to all of the old bosses. "Does this mean we can go now?"

"Rude, always so rude, Russians," Phoenix said under his breath.

I laughed, then winced, forgetting about the bullet in my upper shoulder, and looked over to Junior, pulling the ring from my hand.

"Nope." He held up his hands. "I actually like the early retirement thing, might learn how to golf with my dad."

"You're twenty-six." I pointed out.

He nodded. "One of us has to raise Bam-Bam, plus my dad's still fully running the Nicolasi train wreck."

"YOU IDIOT!" Serena's scream was actually the most terrifying sound ever as she sprinted toward Junior with Bam-Bam chasing happily behind her like they were playing tag.

We all gave Junior a wide berth while King scooped up Bam-Bam and ran in the opposite direction; I mean, it was nearly a full-on sprint, I didn't know he could run that fast.

The rest of the bosses followed, leaving Junior completely abandoned.

"Huh." Nixon laughed. "Bet he wishes he was dead now. She's got a temper."

"Shocked." I smiled over at him, then stopped when his glare was all I received.

"You." He jabbed a finger at me. "Good thinking on making her De Lange. That was smart. You protected her and me, and in the end, you did… good."

I made a face. "On a scale of one to ten, how painful was it to say that out loud, Dad?"

"Fourteen," Nixon grunted. "Wait." He scratched his head. "If she's under De Lange—that means not under Abandonato…"

Oh shit, he was mathing too fast, and I was already injured and losing blood.

"You could touch her—you son of a—"

I started half running, half limping toward her, yelling, "Shield wall." The entire way.

She just blankly stared at me.

"What part of shield wall don't you get?" I roared.

She sidestepped me. "The part where I offer to be your shield when you shot me without warning me."

"Fair," I snapped. "Now save me, tell him I love you or something."

Bella grinned and pointed at me, then yelled to her dad, "Guess who might be a grandpa soon?"

My eyes widened.

"Oh, I'd run if I were you." Bella winked. "Ciao, Ivan."

CHAPTER Thirty-Nine

Let the dead stay that way and let the living—live.
—King Campisi

Ivan

"Come on." I dragged her through the house as much as I could with both of us still recovering from our injuries. "Nobody will notice we're gone."

"You ran into two chairs just to walk me down the hall." She laughed and pressed a kiss to my cheek. We stumbled against the wall in our suite on campus.

We were supposed to be having a party, but everyone was exhausted, even King was yawning like he needed a nap. It had been a week since everything went down.

I think at this point everyone needed therapy after seeing

a ghost like that, and at least the whole white horse missing thing made sense.

Come to find out, one of my men stole it and handed it over to her. She'd been toying with us for a while, bit by bit, until it was time for her big reveal, whatever that was going to be.

I, for one, think she was plagued by guilt and jealousy.

Doctors said she actually suffered some brain damage from her accident-causing severe headaches and paranoia.

It kind of made sense that the part of your brain that feels empathy was more than likely damaged in the process as well.

All she felt was rage.

And now all she'd stare at would be prison walls with nobody to talk to but herself.

"Come on." I pulled open our bedroom door. "They're watching a movie and having wine, they won't even hear us."

"They'll hear you." Bella laughed. "I'm quiet."

"You're not!"

"Last night I—"

"Last night you probably woke up half of the campus."

"They should invest in noise canceling headphones like the rest of our Family does."

She was already pulling her shirt off, and I was already tugging up her skirt, "We'll go super-fast."

"Romantic."

"Desperate." I corrected.

"Ciao, Ivan."

I captured her mouth and ran my hands down her body, cupping her ass, bringing her in against me while she shoved down my briefs. "Ciao, Bella."

All I needed was her.

Maybe we'd establish more rules in our future, maybe we'd make it a thing, but I wasn't so sure they'd be appropriate as I faced her toward the mirror and bent her forward. "I missed you."

"I'm right here."

I sunk into her. "Same, I mean me too, I mean, yes."

"Yes, what?"

"To our Family, to this. I mean yes. I like being a boss, but I think I like being your husband more."

I pressed my hands against hers as she clutched the sink with her hands. "And being a dad, are you open to that?"

"Just don't name him Walt."

"Agreed." She laughed while I wrapped my arms around her and pulled her close. I finally had a home.

And all I had to do was pretend to kill my mentor and best friend to do it.

The mafia was weird, even with our rules it sometimes didn't make sense but in her arms, everything suddenly did.

Blood In. No Out.

EPILOGUE

King

"I have a thought." All of the bosses sat around me, waiting for it, but I wasn't sure how it would be received.

Things were calm, but I had suspicions.

Two of them, to be exact.

Made men.

Brothers that were coming over from Italy to fill in the ranks—mainly to help establish the new rise of the De Lange Family.

They were the best the Nicolasi Family had to offer, recent college graduates, playboys, and brothers.

They also managed to make the news at least once a week and had no respect for anyone but each other and themselves.

They liked women and money. In no specific order.

Ivan groaned. "I don't want them in my Family, they're crazy."

Junior raised his hand. "You agreed to kill me."

"We had a plan!"

"It hurt!"

"YOU TOLD ME TO—"

"Shhhh." Ash waved us off. "I want to hear more about the psychos you decided to bring in, what sort of torture did you have in mind to train them?"

I grinned. "Grunt work, to earn their place."

"Clean up?" Maksim asked.

"Security—for Raven and Tempest."

Ash burst out laughing. "Oh shit, you're serious? Both of them?"

"Well, I figure one will quit pointing out the weak link and the one who stays strong gets to move up the ranks faster." I shrugged. "Simple math."

Maksim shook his head. "Every single person you've put on them has quit, they willingly offer to take bullets for them in an effort to be able to quit their jobs."

"Rumors." I rolled my eyes.

Ash shook his head. "No, I distinctly remember last year when a car exhaust popped the guy said, thank God and moved in front of the twins—with a smile on his face."

Ivan snorted out a laugh. "Poor guy."

"Poor me," Junior grumbled. "I had to take Serena and them shopping the next day and wanted to ram my head through a wall."

It was decided then.

The guys left, and I was alone again in my office. I slowly

walked over to my drawer and grabbed the small horse figurine out of the box.

I'd made additions to it.

Just a small one.

I gave the white horse a stand and engraved on the front of the metal was. "Rise of the De Langes."

A symbol of strength, no longer a symbol of fear.

The End

RESOURCES

If you need to talk to someone, here are some resources that are available all day, every day.
Please know you are not alone.

988 Suicide and Crisis Lifeline

The Lifeline provides 24/7, free and confidential support for people in distress, prevention and crisis resources for you or your loved ones, and best practices for professionals in the United States.
If you or someone you know is having thoughts of suicide or experiencing a mental health or substance use crisis, 988 provides 24/7 connection to confidential support.
There is Hope.
Call or text 988 or chat 988lifeline.org.

Línea de Prevención del Suicidio y Crisis

Lifeline ofrece 24/7, gratuito servicios en español, no es necesario hablar ingles si usted necesita ayuda.
1-888-628-9454

Lifeline Options For Deaf + Hard of Hearing

For TTY Users: Use your preferred relay service or dial 711 then 988.

Veterans Crisis Line
Reach caring, qualified responders with the Department of Veterans Affairs. Many of them are Veterans themselves.
Dial 988 then press
Text: 838255veteranscrisisline.net

Substance Abuse and Mental Health Services Administration (SAMHSA)
SAMHSA's National Helpline is a free, confidential, 24/7, 365-day-a-year treatment referral and information service (in English and Spanish) for individuals and families facing mental and/or substance use disorders prevention, and recovery.
1-800-662-HELP (4357)
TTY: 1-800-487-4889
Text your zip code to: 435748 (HELP4U)
samhsa.gov/find-help/national-helpline
findtreatment.samhsa.gov

WANT MORE RVD?

The Eagle Elite World encompasses a couple of series that can each be read on its own: Eagle Elite (Italian Mafia), Mafia Royals (the next generation), The Rise of the De Langes (the next generation) and Sinacore Family. Pick a couple you want to know more about and enjoy!

Eagle Elite
New Adult, Mafia Romance — Interconnected Standalones

Elite (Nixon & Trace's story)
Elect (Nixon & Trace's story)
Entice (Chase & Mil's story)
Elicit (Tex & Mo's story)
Enamor (Bonus Nixon & Trace story)
Bang Bang (Axton & Amy's story)
Enchant (Frank, Luca & Joyce's story)
Enforce (Elite + from the boys' POV)
Ember (Phoenix & Bee's story)
Elude (Sergio & Andi's story)
Enrapture (Frank, Luca & Joyce's story)
RIP: A Bratva Brotherhood Novel (Nikolai & Maya's story)
Empire (Sergio & Val's story)
Enrage (Dante & El's story)
Eulogy (Chase & Luciana's story)
Envy (Vic & Renee's story)
Debase: A Bratva Brotherhood Novel (Andrei & Alice's story)
Dissolution (Santino & Katya's story)
Exposed (Dom & Tanit's story)

Mafia Royals Romances
Royal Bully (Asher & Claire's story)
Ruthless Princess (Serena & Junior's story
Scandalous Prince (Breaker & Violet's story)
Destructive King (Asher & Annie's story)
Mafia King (Tank & Kartini's story)
Fallen Royal (Maksim & Izzy's story)
Broken Crown (King & Del's story)

Rachel Van Dyken & M. Robinson
Mafia Casanova (Romeo Sinacore's story)
Falling for the Villain (Juliet Sinacore's story)

ACKNOWLEDGEMENTS

There are too many people to thank after writing this book, readers you guys have stayed with me for so long and through so much chaos with my mafia books, welcome home and thank you for continuing to take a chance on me!

It's been a weird and rough few years and it felt so amazing coming home to this book and these characters!

I'm so thankful to God that I can do what I love and also bring you into these crazy mafia worlds and not get judged for all of the emotional damage I cause ;)

Thank you to the husband for grabbing the kids so I could finish this and to Jill and Dani for helping so much with taking over so many things while I focused on deadlines and family! Jill, as always gorgeous cover and formatting, Kay thank you for your epic edits as well as Angie for taking a final pass through.

I truly hope you enjoy this book! I promise there will be more standalones in this series as well as tons of more books releasing in the next eighteen months! ;)

If you want to come hang, my reader group is always open on Facebook Rachel's New Rockin' Readers and follow me on Instagram @RachVD

Happy Reading!

HUGS,
RVD

ABOUT THE AUTHOR

Rachel Van Dyken is the #1 *New York Times*, *Wall Street Journal*, and *USA Today* bestselling author of over 100 books ranging from new adult romance to mafia romance to paranormal & fantasy romance. With over four million copies sold, she's been featured in *Forbes*, *US Weekly*, and *USA Today*. Her books have been translated in more than 15 countries. She was one of the first romance authors to have a Kindle in Motion book through Amazon publishing and continues to strive to be on the cutting edge of the reader experience. She keeps her home in the Pacific Northwest with her husband, adorable sons, naked cat, and two dogs. For more information about her books and upcoming events, visit www.RachelVanDykenAuthor.com.

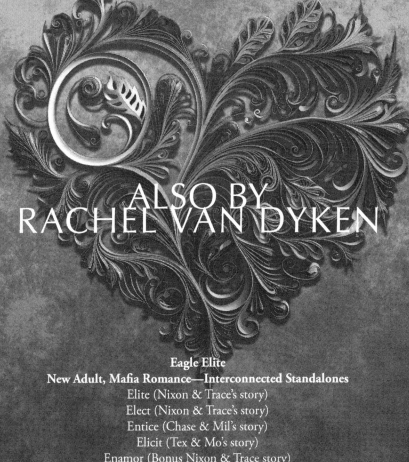

ALSO BY RACHEL VAN DYKEN

Eagle Elite
New Adult, Mafia Romance—Interconnected Standalones
Elite (Nixon & Trace's story)
Elect (Nixon & Trace's story)
Entice (Chase & Mil's story)
Elicit (Tex & Mo's story)
Enamor (Bonus Nixon & Trace story)
Bang Bang (Axton & Amy's story)
Enchant (Frank, Luca & Joyce's story)
Enforce (Elite + from the boys' POV)
Ember (Phoenix & Bee's story)
Elude (Sergio & Andi's story)
Enrapture (Frank, Luca & Joyce's story)
RIP: A Bratva Brotherhood Novel (Nikolai & Maya's story)
Empire (Sergio & Val's story)
Enrage (Dante & El's story)
Eulogy (Chase & Luciana's story)
Envy (Vic & Renee's story)
Debase: A Bratva Brotherhood Novel (Andrei & Alice's story)
Dissolution (Santino & Katya's story)
Exposed (Dom & Tanit's story)

Mafia Royals Romances
New Adult, Mafia Romance—Interconnected Standalones
Royal Bully (Asher & Claire's story)
Ruthless Princess (Serena & Junior's story)
Scandalous Prince (Breaker & Violet's story)
Destructive King (Asher & Annie's story)
Mafia King (Tank & Kartini's story)
Fallen Royal (Maksim & Izzy's story)
Broken Crown (King & Del's story)

Rachel Van Dyken & M. Robinson
New Adult, Romantic Suspense—Interconnected Standalones
Mafia Casanova (Romeo & Eden's story)
Falling for the Villain (Juliet Sinacore's story)

The Dark Ones Saga®
Supernatural Romances—Interconnected Standalones
Dark Origins (Sariel & Nephtal's story)
The Dark Ones (Ethan & Genesis's story)
Untouchable Darkness (Cassius & Stephanie's story)
Dark Surrender (Alex & Hope's story)
Darkest Temptation (Mason & Serenity's story)
Darkest Sinner (Timber & Kyra's story)
Darkest Power (Horus & Kit's story)
Darkest Need (Tarek' & Lilith's story)
Darkest Descent (Bannik's story)

Standalone K-Pop Romances
New Adult, Angsty, Rockstar Romances—Standalone Novels
My Summer In Seoul (Grace's story)
The Anti-Fan & The Idol
Lost in Seoul—written with Colet Abedi (Sookie & Ari's story)

Cruel Summer Trilogy
New Adult, Angsty Romance—Trilogy
Summer Heat (Marlon & Ray's story)
Summer Seduction (Marlon & Ray's story)
Summer Nights (Marlon & Ray's story)

Ruin Series
Mature Young Adult, Angsty Romances—Interconnected Standalones
Ruin (Wes Michels & Kiersten's story)
Toxic (Gabe Hyde & Saylor's story)
Fearless (Wes Michels & Kiersten's story)
Shame (Tristan & Lisa's story)

Seaside Series
Young Adult, Angsty, Rockstar Romances—Interconnected Standalones
Tear (Alec, Demetri & Natalee's story)
Pull (Demetri & Alyssa's story)
Shatter (Alec & Natalee's story)
Forever (Alec & Natalee's story)
Fall (Jamie Jaymeson & Pricilla's story)
Strung (Tear+ from the boys' POV)
Eternal (Demetri & Alyssa's story)

Seaside Pictures
New Adult, Dramedy, Celebrity Romances—Interconnected Standalones
Capture (Lincoln & Dani's story)
Keep (Zane & Fallon's story)
Steal (Will & Angelica's story)
All Stars Fall (Trevor & Penelope's story)
Abandon (Ty & Abigail's story)
Provoke (Braden & Piper's story)
Surrender (Drew & Bronte's story)

Standalone Romances
New Adult, Angsty Romance—Standalone Novels
The Perfects (Ambrose & Mary-Belle's story)
The Unperfects (Quinn's story)

Players Game
New Adult, Sports Romances—Interconnected Standalones
Fraternize (Miller, Grant and Emerson's story)
Infraction (Miller & Kinsey's story)
M.V.P. (Jax & Harley's story)

The EX Files
New Adult, Romantic Comedies—Interconnected Standalones
Exposing the Groom (Killian & Scarlett's story)

Covet
New Adult, Angsty Romances—Interconnected Standalones
Stealing Her (Bridge & Isobel's story)
Finding Him (Julian & Keaton's story)

The Bet Series
New Adult, Romantic Comedies—Interconnected Standalones
The Bet (Travis & Kacey's story)
The Wager (Jake & Char Lynn's story)
The Love Strategy— previously titled The Dare (Jace & Beth Lynn's story)
Love Hazard

The Bachelors of Arizona
New Adult Romances—Interconnected Standalones
The Bachelor Auction (Brock & Jane's story)
The Playboy Bachelor (Bentley & Margot's story)
The Bachelor Contract (Brant & Nikki's story)

The Consequence Series
New Adult, Laugh Out Loud RomComs—Interconnected Standalones
The Consequence of Loving Colton (Colton & Milo's story)
The Consequence of Revenge (Max & Becca's story)
The Consequence of Seduction (Reid & Jordan's story)
The Consequence of Rejection (Jason & Maddy's story)

The Emory Games
New Adult, Laugh Out Loud RomComs—Standalone Novels
Office Hate (Mark & Olivia's story)
Office Date (Jack & Ivy's story)
Office Mate (Ace & Bri's story)

Red Card
New Adult, Sports Romances—Interconnected Standalones
Risky Play (Slade & Mackenzie's story)
Kickin' It (Matt & Parker's story)

Wingmen Inc.
New Adult, Romantic Comedies—Interconnected Standalones
The Matchmaker's Playbook (Ian & Blake's story)
The Matchmaker's Replacement (Lex & Gabi's story)

Bro Code
New Adult Romance—Standalone Novels
Co-Ed (Knox & Shawn's story)
Seducing Mrs. Robinson (Leo & Kora's story)
Avoiding Temptation (Slater & Tatum's story)
The Setup (Finn & Jillian's story)

Liars, Inc
New Adult, Romantic Comedies—Interconnected Standalones
Dirty Exes (Colin, Jessie & Blaire's story)
Dangerous Exes (Jessie & Isla's story)

Curious Liaisons
New Adult, Romantic Comedies—Interconnected Standalones
Cheater (Lucas & Avery's story)
Cheater's Regret (Thatch & Austin's story)

Standalone Dramedy
RomCom with Dramatic Moments—Standalone Novel
The Godparent Trap (Rip & Colby's story)

Kathy Ireland & Rachel Van Dyken
Women's Fiction— Standalone
Fashion Jungle

Rachel Van Dyken & Patti Stanger
New Adult, Fantasy Romance—Standalone
Compel (Ben & Luna's story)

Holiday Romances
Romantic Comedies, Royal Romances—Standalone Novel
A Crown for Christmas (Fitz & Phillipa's story)
We Three Kings (Zautland & Samira's story)

Standalone Romances
New Adult, Romantic Comedies—Standalone Novels
Every Girl Does It (Preston & Amanda's story)
Compromising Kessen (Christian & Kessen's story)

New Adult, Fantasy Romance—Standalone Novel
Divine Uprising (Athena & Adonis's story)

Inspirational, Historical Romance—Standalone Novel
The Parting Gift—written with Leah Sanders (Blaine and Mara's story)

Waltzing With The Wallflower—written with Leah Sanders
Regency Romances—Interconnected Standalones
Waltzing with the Wallflower (Ambrose & Cordelia)
Beguiling Bridget (Anthony & Bridget's story)
Taming Wilde (Colin & Gemma's story)

London Fairy Tales
Fairy Tale Inspired Regency Romances—Interconnected Standalones
Upon a Midnight Dream (Stefan & Rosalind's story)
Whispered Music (Dominique & Isabelle's story)
The Wolf's Pursuit (Hunter & Gwendolyn's story)
When Ash Falls (Ashton & Sofia's story)

Renwick House
Regency Romances—Interconnected Standalones
The Ugly Duckling Debutante (Nicholas & Sara's story)
The Seduction of Sebastian St. James (Sebastian & Emma's story)
The Redemption of Lord Rawlings (Phillip & Abigail's story)
An Unlikely Alliance (Royce & Evelyn's story)
The Devil Duke Takes a Bride (Benedict & Katherine's story)

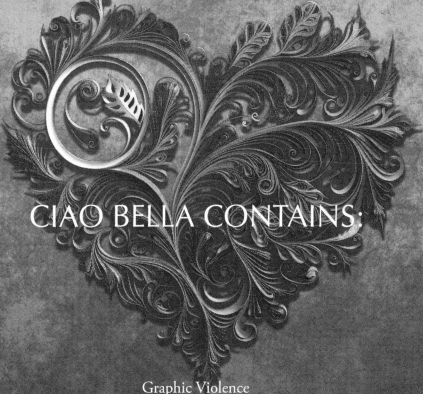

CIAO BELLA CONTAINS:

Graphic Violence
Forced Marriage
Murder
Depression
Character experiences brief moments of suicidal thoughts

Printed in Poland
by Amazon Fulfillment
Poland Sp. z o.o., Wrocław